Acclaim for

"Utterly hot, intense, fierce, and passionate, Ms. Carew's writing style is amazing. Top pick!"

—*The Romance Reviews*

"Opal Carew is a genius at spinning the most erotic stories by tapping into forbidden fantasies and visiting emotions that bring the characters literally to their knees. A steamy-hot read!" —*Fresh Fiction* on *Pleasure Bound*

"Carew definitely knows how to turn up the heat, and her descriptions of the physical and mental aspects of BDSM are spot-on. . . . This book deserves a spot on top of your to-be-read pile." —*RT BookReviews* on *Secret Ties*

"A blazing-hot erotic romp . . . a must-read for lovers of erotic romance. A fabulously fun and stupendously steamy read for a cold winter's night. This one's so hot, you might need to wear oven mitts while you're reading it!"

—*Romance Junkies* on *Swing*

"Carew's book reminds me of a really good box of chocolates that you want to savor, but can't help eating all up in one sitting because it's so decadent and yummy. Feast on this one today!" —*Night Owl Romance* on *Bliss*

"A hot book that will have you panting for more. The fantasies that the characters play out are guilty pleasures that will leave you breathless. I think Opal Carew definitely knows what she is writing about. If you like steamy sex, hot men, steamy sex, hot women, steamy sex, multiple partners, steamy sex, role-playing, and steamy sex then you will want to read this hot novel! Oh . . . did I mention the steamy sex?" —*Coffee Time Romance* on *Bliss*

"Delicious in its sensuality. Opal Carew has a great imagination and her sensual scenes are sure to get a fire going in many readers." —*A Romance Review* on *Twin Fantasies*

"Humor, angst, drama, lots of hot sex, and interesting characters make for an entertaining read that you will have a hard time putting down."
—*The Romance Studio* on *Twin Fantasies*

"There is little chance of reading anything more sexually stimulating than a book by Opal Carew. Her characters in this story are not only adventurous lovers, but are fun loving and sweet during every encounter . . . and that makes this story such a pleasure to read. I really enjoy the lighthearted banter and sizzling sexuality of these two lovers as well as their very sexy friends."
—*Coffee Time Romance* on *Total Abandon*

"Opal Carew brings erotic romance to a whole new level. . . . She sets your senses on fire!" —*Reader to Reader*

"Smoking-hot sex and intense MC alpha heroes. Get ready to ride!"
—*New York Times* bestselling author Carly Phillips

"The constant and imaginative sexual situations along with the likable characters with emotional depth keep the reader's interest. Be prepared for all manner of coupling including groups, exhibitionism, voyeurism, and same-sex unions. . . . I recommend *Swing* for the adventuresome who don't mind singeing their senses."

—*Regency Reader*

"Written with great style . . . a must for any erotic romance fan, ménage enthusiasts in particular."

—*Just Erotic Romance Reviews* on *Twin Fantasies*

"Carew pulls off another scorcher. . . . She knows how to write a love scene that takes her reader to dizzying heights of pleasure." —*My Romance Story*

"So much fun to read . . . The story line is fast-paced with wonderful humor. Opal Carew provides a fabulous heater." —*Genre Go Round Reviews*

"Opal Carew has given these characters depth and realism. . . . *Twin Fantasies* is a thrilling romance, full of both incredible passion and heart-warming tenderness, and Opal Carew is an author to watch."

—*Joyfully Reviewed*

ALSO BY OPAL CAREW

Riding Steele

Opal Carew

ST. MARTIN'S GRIFFIN

NEW YORK

RIDING STEELE. Copyright © 2015 by Opal Carew. All rights reserved. Printed in the United States of America. For information, address St. Martin's Press, 175 Fifth Avenue, New York, N.Y. 10010.

www.stmartins.com

The following chapters in this book were previously published as individual e-books.
Riding Steele #1: Kidnapped. Copyright © 2014 by Opal Carew.
Riding Steele #2: Untamed. Copyright © 2014 by Opal Carew.
Riding Steele #3: Collide. Copyright © 2014 by Opal Carew.
Riding Steele #4: Wanted. Copyright © 2014 by Opal Carew.
Riding Steele #5: Crossroads. Copyright © 2014 by Opal Carew.
Riding Steele #6: Aftershock. Copyright © 2014 by Opal Carew.

Library of Congress Cataloging-in-Publication Data

Carew, Opal.
    Riding Steele / Opal Carew. — First edition.
        pages ; cm
    ISBN 978-1-250-05284-1 (trade paperback)
    ISBN 978-1-4668-5470-3 (e-book)
    I. Title.
    II.
    PR9199.4.C367R63 2015
    813'.6—dc23

                                                    2014044285

St. Martin's Griffin books may be purchased for educational, business, or promotional use. For information on bulk purchases, please contact the Macmillan Corporate and Premium Sales Department at 1-800-221-7945, extension 5442, or write to specialmarkets@macmillan.com.

First Edition: March 2015

10 9 8 7 6 5 4 3 2 1

To Laurie,
aka the Tempest,
my dear friend,
who is creative, genuinely romantic,
and provides me with
great inspiration!

Acknowledgments

Thank you to Rose Hilliard, my fabulous editor. Thank you to Emily Sylvan Kim, my wonderful agent. Thanks to my husband, Mark, and my sons, Matt and Jason, for always being so supportive of my work. Thank you to Laurie, who helps me with so many things. And a special thank-you to Katy Cartwright, for designing the adorable Bebe, the biker babe!

Riding Steele

Kidnapped

"Is that the woman Killer's friend wants us to kidnap?"

Steele glanced in the direction Shock was looking. Steele and his men were sitting in a pub called Big Rigg that had heavy wooden tables and a rustic atmosphere. A woman walked toward one of the high tables at the bar where a suited man and a couple were sitting. He recognized the newcomer from the pictures of Craig's sister that Killer had shown him.

They didn't do her justice.

Steele nodded. "That's the one."

Her name was Laurie and she was stunning. Long, glossy, dark brown hair that careened loosely over her shoulders, beautiful big eyes, a pert nose, and lips that begged to be kissed. And her body. Damn! Every heart-stopping curve was showcased in her short, snug, black dress. His eyes followed the long, slim line of her torso to the arc of her hips, then down the longest legs he'd ever seen. Slim and shapely, ending in glossy black stilettos studded with rhinestones. How she could walk in those heels—which had to be at least six inches high—he didn't know, but every man in the bar must be thanking his lucky stars at the sight of her glorious swaying ass. He allowed his gaze to make a leisurely climb upward before stopping at her breasts. Round, firm, and snugly cocooned in the tight black dress.

The hint of cleavage in the deep-V neckline caused his body to tighten. His fingers itched to wrap around those glorious breasts. To feel the softness in his hands. To stroke the nipples with his thumbs.

Fuck, his cock was swelling painfully in his jeans.

But this was someone's sister. Craig, Killer's friend. And Craig wanted to protect her.

Steele knew what that felt like. Thoughts of Chrissy shattered his mood. Dead at eighteen. Pain slashed through him. No matter how much Steele had tried to protect his younger sister, had tried to steer her from hanging out with the wrong crowd, headstrong Chrissy had ignored his sage advice and done whatever the hell she'd damned well pleased. And died of a drug overdose.

Now he'd been offered a chance to help another brother save his sister from a bad situation. He had been fucking tempted to do exactly what Craig had drunkenly suggested when they'd partied together with Killer the night before, but Steele drew the line at kidnapping.

Raven leaned close to Rip. "What are they talking about? Are we going to kidnap someone?" She grinned. "Is that part of Steele's birthday celebration?"

"No," Rip answered. "When we were drinking with Killer yesterday, he introduced us to a friend who kinda asked us to kidnap his sister. She's been dating this guy and he's concerned about her. He left to go out of town today, but he has a bad feeling. He wanted us to keep her safe until he gets back."

"I think he just wanted to get her out of the picture for a while," Shock said, "to make the guy think she's dumped him, hoping he'd move on to another woman."

"That's crazy." Raven sipped her beer. "The sister would never forgive him and the minute she got back, she'd go find the boyfriend and explain."

"He's desperate," Steele said. "For some reason, he thinks this guy is really bad news. He's trying to protect his sister, and I get that. But we're not kidnapping her."

Raven eyed the well-groomed man in the expensive suit standing beside Laurie at the bar.

"He looks like the kind of guy most brothers would want their sisters involved with. He dresses well and probably makes a good living."

She grinned at Steele. "I'm actually surprised Killer's friend would want her in your hands rather than his. Wouldn't he worry that she'd be in danger of being man-handled by you and the rest of your crew?" She started fanning herself with a big grin on her face. "Whew! Is it getting hot in here?"

"I don't understand either," said Steele. "I got the impression he's close with Killer, and since Killer vouched for us and the guy has no other options, he was willing to take a chance. Then again, the guy could be stupid and crazy, which is why I don't want to get too wrapped up in this mess."

"Well, I think we should do it. I'm all for having another chick around." Shock stared at the woman's ass. "Especially one as gorgeous as that."

"Are you tired of me already, Shock?" Raven asked.

He grinned. "Never, babe. But access is limited with this possessive man of yours." He nodded toward Rip.

Steele laughed. Rip was pretty generous with his woman.

"Even if we did kidnap her, which is *not* going to happen, it wouldn't be like that," Steele said. "She'd be under our protection. *My* protection. Right?"

They all muttered in affirmation, but it was all for show. None of these men would force themselves on a woman. And it was moot anyway.

He had decided to come here tonight to check out the situation, though. He could at least do that much. And keep an eye on her, from a distance, until her brother, Craig, got back in town.

"So, Steele, now that we've satisfied Killer's friend's request and checked that the sister's okay," Shock said, "how about we get on with celebrating your birthday?"

"We've got time for one more beer before we go meet Dom and Magic." Steele hailed the waitress.

Laurie sat on the stool beside Donovan, tugging on the hem of the short black dress. He had sent it to her this afternoon, along with the death-defying heels, insisting she wear the outfit tonight for their six-month anniversary.

She felt overdressed for this pub, but Donovan liked it here. It had its own microbrewery and Donovan was partial to a black lager they specialized in, as well as a stout with undertones of bitter sweet chocolate. She also suspected he liked being in a place where he and his wealth stood out from the average person.

Donovan's friends Joan and Henry sat across the small rectangular bar table from them.

She hated being on display like this, and she hated feeling outside her depth with a man, but Donovan's controlling nature kept her off-balance and unsure of herself, even though in all other areas of her life, she'd always been strong and independent.

That's why she'd decided that tonight she would end it. Well, she *had* decided that, but when he'd announced they were celebrating an anniversary, she'd decided she should wait a few days.

He picked up his glass containing a beer as dark as cola, and finished the last of it, then pushed it aside. He slid his arm around her waist and pulled her tight to his body. She tried not to cringe, but he noticed the slight tensing of her body, so he pulled her tighter.

"I know it was a surprise that Joan and Henry are joining us for a drink, love, but I promise it won't be all evening. They just wanted to toast our anniversary and wish us well. Surely you don't mind?"

"No, of course not." She smiled at Joan. Laurie hardly

knew either of them, but Henry was an old friend of
Donovan's.

In fact, she was glad they had joined them. She didn't
really want to be alone with Donovan. Their relationship
had been getting more and more out of control, as he became more demanding and . . . well, almost abusive.

She knew she had to break it off, but he was . . . intimidating.

A waitress arrived at the table and set flute glasses in
front of each of them and a barman arrived with a bottle
of champagne—Dom Pérignon, no less. He popped the
cork, then filled each of their glasses.

Donovan lifted his glass. "To a wonderful anniversary,
and many more."

Laurie lifted her glass and clinked it against the others,
feeling like a total liar. She wanted out of this relationship
as fast as she could get out.

But she sipped her wine.

"Now for your gift." Donovan reached into his pocket
and removed a long, velvet box adorned with a small shiny
gold bow. Instead of handing it to her, he snapped it open
and showed it to her. Diamonds glittered against the dark
blue velvet lining of the box.

"Oh, it's beautiful," Joan exclaimed. "Is it a bracelet?"

"It's a necklace." Donovan lifted the sparkling gift from
its nest of velvet. It was four rows of stunning diamonds
wide. "Let me put it on you."

She knew there was no point in arguing. He would
win and she would come off looking unappreciative
and spoiled.

She lifted her hair and he wrapped the necklace around her neck, then fastened it.

It was more a collar than a necklace, hugging her neck closely. She felt like she would choke from it. It reminded her of the last time they'd made love, if you could call it that, when his fingers had wrapped around her throat in a choking hold as he'd thrust into her from behind. Her wrists had been chained, so she couldn't push away his hands, and when she'd tried to protest, he'd tightened his hold until she couldn't utter words. The only sound she could make were just whimpers of frustration.

She had almost fainted as he'd taken his own pleasure and left her gasping for breath.

Before that, his dominant sexual demands had pushed her limits in ways she hadn't liked, but that time had shown her he could be dangerous. And it had become crystal clear that he cared not a whit about her pleasure.

She gazed at him. "Thank you."

She could tell he knew she was thinking about the other night, and he smiled. He loved wielding control over her. Instead of drawing his hands away from her neck, his fingertips stroked the front of her throat. She half expected him to wrap his other hand around her neck and squeeze until she lost consciousness. But that was foolish. He would never do anything like that . . . in public.

Still, she had trouble breathing normally. He dragged his fingertips along the edge of the necklace, then drew her hair back from her shoulder.

"What do you think, Joan?" he asked, his hand resting on Laurie's shoulder.

Joan stared at Laurie's neck with obvious admiration, and a touch of jealousy. "It's absolutely stunning. You're a lucky girl, Laurie."

Donovan smiled. "And I'm sure she'll show me her gratitude later tonight."

He said it in a light tone, the kind any guy might use while making a joking innuendo, and everyone laughed, but Laurie knew better. He expected her to thank him properly, and thoroughly. And if she didn't meet his expectations, he would punish her.

And even if she did . . .

He leaned in and nuzzled her neck. "I can hardly wait." The hand on her shoulder slid to the base of her neck and he squeezed, reminding her of what he liked.

Wild Card grabbed another handful of the nachos covered in meat, cheese, and salsa, and dropped them onto his plate.

"Why bother with the plate? You're going to be finishing those on your own." Shock tossed back the rest of the beer in his glass and stood up.

"You guys really going?" Wild Card asked.

"We told you we were leaving after this beer, but you pulled a typical Card Trick and ordered them."

"I'm not finished with my beer."

Steele chuckled as he stood up, too. "That makes one of us. Just join us later, man."

The others all stood up except Rip, who was staring across the bar.

"You coming?" Raven ran her hand over his shoulder affectionately and squeezed.

Rip dragged his gaze from the woman in the black dress across the bar to look at Raven. "Yeah, of course, baby."

But then he turned and leaned close to Wild Card. "Look, keep an eye on her, okay?"

"Why? What's up?" Wild Card asked.

"Something's not right. The guy just gave her an expensive-looking necklace, but she doesn't seem too happy about it. And check out the dress. She's not comfortable in that or the shoes."

Wild Card glanced at the woman who was staring at her tall stemmed glass. He had seen when the guy had flashed a box with a glittering necklace inside and then fastened it around the woman's neck, but he hadn't noticed anything out of the ordinary. She hadn't bubbled all over the guy, but some women were more subdued in their reactions. He hadn't thought anything of it. But Rip, he was an ex-cop and he could read people. If he said there was something wrong, Wild Card wouldn't question it.

And he didn't question why Rip would suggest he keep an eye on her. Steele had taken an interest in her, for whatever reason, so that put her under Steele's protection. That meant she was also under the protection of every man who rode with Steele.

Wild Card nodded and Rip stood up, then followed Raven toward the door.

Wild Card watched the woman as he ate his nachos.

She was hot as all get-out, and that body-hugging dress
was spectacular, but he now noticed little things that made
him understand why Rip had said she was uncomfortable
in it. She kept discreetly tugging on the hem, and under
the table she would slip her foot from one of the high-
heeled shoes and rub it against her slender ankle, then slide
it back again. Clearly, she was itching to be out of them.

Damn, but they were so sexy. He wanted to think
she loved wearing them, and that she loved the attention
of every man's gaze on the sway of her shapely ass as she
walked in them.

He wished Steele hadn't vetoed kidnapping the woman.
Kidnapping her didn't mean bedding her, but who knows?
Maybe she'd be turned on by being surrounded by a gang
of bikers and she'd decide she wanted to put out.

Raven sure hadn't been the type he'd have figured to
get involved with the whole gang of them, but she'd surprised them all. And she was one hot fuck. Who knew with
this woman?

"No, thanks," Laurie said as Donovan tipped the champagne bottle to her glass to refill it, but he ignored her.

He filled it to the top, then added to Joan's and Henry's
glasses, but only filling them a quarter before pouring
the last bit into his own.

He lifted his glass. "To my beautiful woman." The
others raised their glasses and clinked and she reluctantly
joined them. She didn't want any more champagne. It went
straight to her head and she wanted to keep her wits about

her. But as she sipped, Donovan subtly nudged her arm to deepen the sip.

He glanced at his watch. "Aren't you two going to be late for your play?"

"We've got plenty of time," Henry answered.

"But, honey," Joan said with a smile, "I'm sure these two lovebirds would like to be alone." She tipped back her glass and swallowed the rest of her wine.

"All right. I get it." Henry finished his and stood up, then pulled back Joan's stool. "You two have a great evening." He winked, then followed Joan to the door.

"Drink up," Donovan said.

She stared at her glass, still three quarters full. "I really don't want anymore."

"I said, drink it." His tone brooked no argument and, hating herself for it, she obeyed and lifted her glass.

She took a sip, then as his dark gaze bored through her, she tipped back the rest of the glass. Damn, why didn't she just say no and walk away? But there was something about him and his intimidating way. He hadn't started out this way. He used to be kind, generous, and thoughtful. But the more she got to know him, the more his dark side came out. And as much as she hated it, when he used his controlling, authoritative tone, she fell into line. She barely even knew herself when she became like this. Letting a man control her.

She had to stop this. Anniversary or not, she had to put an end to this unhealthy relationship.

She drew in a deep breath, steeling her courage.

"Donovan, I was going to wait until after our anniversary to do this but . . ."

She hesitated at the stormy look in his eyes, but then pushed herself to continue.

"This relationship isn't working for me. I'm just not the kind of woman you're looking for—"

"Shut up." The hard words came out in a low tone that no one nearby would hear, but they rocked through her.

He pulled out his phone and texted something, then grabbed a roll of bills from his pocket and dropped two hundreds on the table. He grasped her upper arm and squeezed painfully, then stood up and guided her through the restaurant to the door.

She was having trouble keeping up with him in the ridiculously high heels and stumbled. Donovan jerked her back to her feet.

A nearby waiter paused. "Are you all right, ma'am?"

"She's fine," Donovan answered for her. "She'd just had a little too much to drink."

Her cheeks flushed, not wanting people to think she was drunk, but her red cheeks only added credence to his words.

The waiter nodded. "Well, good evening, sir. Ma'am." Then he continued on his way.

When they stepped out the door, Donovan tugged her along with him down the sidewalk and through a glass door to the parking garage next to the bar. He jabbed the button for the elevator. Another couple was approaching so she didn't bring up their conversation again.

"We're not taking the limo?" she asked. Donovan had been drinking and the idea of getting into a car with him made her nervous.

"No, I brought the 'vette."

She wanted to protest, but she knew it would do no good. In fact, the more she protested, the more likely he was to drive recklessly, just to scare her.

The other couple followed them into the elevator and they rode it down to P2. Donovan slid his arm around her waist and when the doors opened, he guided her forward. The door closed on the other couple behind them.

"Donovan, I know you're upset, but we need to talk about this."

But he walked faster through the cavernous parking garage, her shoes clacking against the concrete floor. He held her elbow now and she raced to keep up with him, her feet aching in the high-heeled shoes, barely stopping herself from toppling over.

"Where are we going?" she asked as they kept on walking. Where there had been lots of cars parked near the elevator, as they continued, the empty parking spaces were more plentiful, until finally there were almost no cars around at all.

A quiver ran down her spine at how isolated she felt. Relieved, she saw his sleek, black, vintage Corvette parked ahead. Once in the car, she could talk. Even though she didn't want to be in the car while he was driving, at least he would have to listen. He might not like that she was breaking free of his control by breaking up with him, but what could he really do about it? He couldn't force her up to his apartment, and there's no way she was going with him of her own free will.

She breathed a sigh of relief as they approached the car, but that relief was short-lived as he turned suddenly and thrust her against a big, concrete post, knocking the wind from her. Her clutch purse fell from her hands and she instinctively went to pick it up, but he shoved her back again and slapped her hard across the face. She stared up at him, dazed, her cheek stinging.

"What the fuck are you thinking?" His dark eyes glinted in anger as he glared at her. "*You* don't end it with me. If and when we end this relationship, it will be because *I* decide to end it. When I'm tired of you." His face jerked close to hers. "Do you understand?"

At his harsh, uncompromising tone, she found herself nodding. Her stomach twisted.

Oh, God, what am I doing? I can't let him get away with treating me like this.

But fear kept her from arguing with him. She was alone and isolated and she really didn't know what he would do if she didn't do as she was told.

He pulled her into an aggressive kiss, his tongue driving deep into her mouth. Her jaw ached as he forced it wide with his thrusts, then she felt his hand glide up her thigh. She pressed her hand against his chest to push him away. His fingers slid under her dress and stroked the crotch of her panties. Panic vaulted through her and she pushed against him.

Somehow she got her mouth free. "No." But no matter how hard she pushed, she couldn't budge him. He was bigger and stronger than she was and she felt totally helpless. She wanted to scream, but he thrust his body tighter against hers, crushing her to the concrete pillar, then he grabbed her face and took her lips again. As his tongue drove inside her again, his fingers pulled at the elastic of her panties.

She shivered, knowing he was going to take her right here in the garage.

"I think the lady would like you to leave her alone."

Donovan pulled his mouth away and glared at her, shriveling the budding idea she had to call to the other man for help. Without turning around, his gaze still locked with hers, he said sharply, "Get lost. This is none of your business."

"I'm making it my business."

It was all Wild Card could do not to grab the guy and pull him off her. As soon as he'd seen the guy practically drag the woman from the bar, he'd known there was trouble brewing. He'd followed them from the bar, then taken the stairs to catch up to them. As he'd been crossing the garage, he'd seen the guy slap her across the face. Now he had the obviously frightened woman pinned against a pillar and he was mauling her. Wild Card's heart pounded as protective instincts surged through him.

The guy finally turned. At six foot two, Wild Card knew he made an intimidating sight, especially with his leather jacket and studded riding gloves.

The other man straightened, sizing up his opponent. "You don't get it. She loves this. Pretending to be taken in an alleyway or a parking garage, that gets her off. Especially if she can fight it." He turned to her. "Right, sweetheart?"

She said nothing, and he laughed and stroked her cheek. "And she loves to play timid."

Wild Card's hands clenched as the man turned back to face him.

"I don't believe you," Wild Card said.

The guy's eyes narrowed as he stared at Wild Card, then he shrugged and smiled.

"Tell you what. I'll give you a thousand dollars to fuck her. Right here, right now." He grinned. "And I remember seeing you in the bar with a bunch of friends. Why don't you call them in, too, and you can all have a go? A real gangbang." He had a nasty glitter in his eyes. "I know she would love that."

"Really?" Wild Card raised an eyebrow and stepped closer, looking interested. "And what would you be doing?" he asked.

He turned back to the woman and his gaze glided down her body. "I'd just watch."

Wild Card finally allowed the anger and contempt he felt to show on his face.

"Then why the fuck do we need you?"

He drew back his fist and slugged the sleazy face of the asshole, knocking him back against his shiny, sleek car, then he grabbed him by the shoulders, pulled him back to his feet, and slugged him again. This time he left him in a heap on the ground.

He grabbed the woman's hand. "Come on."

He drew her along, but she couldn't go fast in those heels, so he scooped her over his shoulder and carried her.

"No, please, just let me go."

"And when Asshole here wakes up, what do you think he'll do to you?"

Luckily, his bike wasn't parked too far away. He plopped her on the seat. It was better to have his passenger behind him, but he didn't want her jumping off at a light, so he had her in front. She was frightened and panicky and might do something stupid.

"Here, put this on." He handed her his spare helmet.

"No, I—"

"Don't argue." He pushed it onto her head and buckled it, then pulled on his own helmet and started up the bike.

He took off down the street. Fuck, he had no idea what he was going to do with this woman, but he knew that taking her to her home was the worst thing to do. Once that guy woke up, he'd probably go straight to find her and take out his anger on her.

There was only one thing he could do. He turned onto the highway and headed into the night.

Laurie shivered as the bike sped along the highway.

First, Donovan had nearly raped her in the parking garage, then—God, she still couldn't believe it—had offered her to a bunch of bikers to be gang raped. The biker had knocked Donavon out, and kidnapped her. Now he was probably taking her back to where his gang was, to . . .

She choked back a sob, not wanting to think about what they'd do to her.

And, idiot that she was, she almost felt protected within the confines of his strong arms. He'd seemed to show concern about what Donovan would do to her once he woke up, but she knew she was just looking for a knight in shining armor—or leather, in this case—to save the day. But she had to rely on herself. Allowing a man any kind of control over her, even to save her, was a big mistake. It was a lesson she'd learned from Donovan that she would never forget.

They pulled off the highway and rode along a long curved road. They'd been traveling for about a half hour. She shivered uncontrollably now, as much from the cold as from fear. The man must have felt her trembling because he tightened his arm around her waist and pulled her tighter to his solid, muscular chest. She didn't fight. Just rested back against him, saving her energy for what would come.

Twenty minutes later, he turned onto a smaller road and wound through the trees until they reached an unpaved road. He drove along the gravel surface until they finally pulled up to a clearing where a large log house stood. He stopped the bike in front of the house.

He unfastened his helmet and pulled it off. As he dismounted the bike, she began to shiver again, then realized she'd stopped trembling for a while when his arm had been wrapped around her. The warmth of his body had helped. He reached for the strap under her chin and un-fastened it, then tugged the helmet from her head.

He lifted her from the bike like she weighed nothing and set her on her feet. He was big, tattooed, and dangerous-looking, with hazel eyes and dark blond hair spiked on top and short on the sides.

Her heart pounded in her chest. Her hands clenched into fists, feeling empty without her small clutch purse, which must still be lying on the ground in the parking garage. With her cell phone inside.

"Come on." He took her hand and led her toward the house. They stepped from the dirt surface, where the bike was parked, to grass. It was difficult walking because the tiny tips of her stiletto heels kept digging into the soil. She stumbled and the man grasped her elbow, keeping her steady. Unlike Donovan, he moved at a slow enough pace so that she could keep her balance and keep up with him.

He opened the front door and led her inside. It was dark and she couldn't see much of the place. Just shadowy shapes of furniture illuminated by moonlight coming in the windows.

"Please, just let me go," she pleaded.

"Look, I'm not going to hurt you. I promise you that."

He led her forward, then turned on a light over a stair-way.

She shook her head. "How can I? You just kidnapped me."

"I saved you from a douche bag."

He guided her up the stairs, his big hand pressed to

the small of her back, and then they walked down the hall-way past several doors. He stopped at the door at the end of the hallway, then he opened it.

He flicked on the light and her eyes widened as she saw a big bed in the center of the room.

"No, please." She tried to pull away from him, but he grabbed her arm.

"I told you, I'm not going to hurt you." His mouth compressed into a flat line. "But you're not going to believe that." He scowled. "Okay, come with me."

Hope sprang through her that maybe he was going to let her go, but then he opened another door and her heart sank as she saw it was another bedroom. He went to the bedside table, with her still in tow, and opened the drawer, then drew something out.

Handcuffs.

She began to struggle as he tugged her back to the other room again, and his strong hand tightened around her wrist. Then cold steel flashed across her skin as he fastened a cuff around her wrist. He dragged her toward the bed.

"No," she wailed, shaking her head wildly. Tears prick-led at her eyes.

The last time she'd had sex with Donovan, he'd con-vinced her to let him handcuff her, then he'd wrapped his hands around her throat and squeezed until she'd almost fainted. She was sure what she would experience with this big, rough biker would be far worse than anything Donovan had done to her.

"Look, I just need you to stay here," he said. "We're a

long way out, and if you bolt, especially in the middle
of the night, you could get hurt."

He fastened the other cuff around one of the posts of
the headboard, then he pulled back the big comforter on
the bed. "Get in."

She bit her lower lip, but lay down on the bed. He
reached for her ankle and she stiffened, but he just pulled
off first one shoe, then the other one, and dropped them on
the floor, then he covered her with the comforter.

"Just get some sleep. We'll talk about this in the morning when you've had time to calm down."

He stepped back and she just stared at him, sucking in
big breaths. He walked to the door and opened it, then
paused and turned back to her.

"I'm sorry about this."

Then he turned out the light and closed the door
behind him.

Steele pulled up in front of the cabin Killer had arranged
for them to stay at while they were here. It belonged to
his brother who was out of the country for the summer,
but allowed Killer to use it whenever he liked.

Steele dismounted his bike, then pulled off his helmet.
It had been an enjoyable evening carousing around the
town. They'd eaten in a little hole-in-the-wall restaurant
with only a handful of tables, but it had the best burger
he'd ever eaten. Killer had recommended the place when
Rip had told him how much Steele loved his burgers.

Afterward, the guys had insisted on taking him to a

strip club. When they'd first suggested it, he was worried Raven would be uncomfortable, but he should have known better than that by now. The woman seemed up for pretty much anything. In fact, he was surprised she hadn't starting stuffing bills in strippers' G-strings.

He was pretty sure it had fired her up, though. On the way back, as he watched Rip riding behind him in his rearview mirror, he was pretty sure she was stroking Rip's cock through his jeans as they drove. Seeing that, after watching the naked gyrating women at the club, had him pretty fucking hot, too. He hoped that now that they were back at the cabin, Raven would be up for a good fuck with all of them. Or even a special birthday fuck just for him.

But when Raven climbed off Rip's bike, Rip tugged her into a deep kiss, his hands cupping her round ass and pulling her tight to him. Then he grabbed her hand and pulled her toward the door. Steele and the others followed them inside.

"See you guys tomorrow," Rip said as the two of them scurried up the stairs.

Rip had met Raven when they'd passed through his hometown for a wedding a few weeks ago, and he'd fallen head over heels for her. Her real name was Hayley, but Rip had dubbed her Raven because of her glossy black hair, and the name had stuck.

Steele had never seen Rip happier, and Raven seemed to be living on cloud nine, too. She had blossomed since she'd joined them a few weeks ago, and Steele had a feeling she'd be around for quite a while.

He sighed and walked into the kitchen, then grabbed himself a glass of water and downed it. Not as good as a cold shower, but it helped his parched throat.

Shock grabbed a few beers from the fridge. "Want one, birthday boy?"

Steele leaned against the counter, his cock aching. "Naw. What I want requires an available female."

Shock chuckled. "You and me both. Too bad Raven and Rip took off so fast." He shrugged. "But they deserve alone time, too."

No one could argue that both Rip and Raven weren't generous with her favors.

"That's the truth." Steele filled his glass again, halfway, then downed it.

"Well, the guys and I are going to play some cards. I'd ask you to join us, but maybe the best thing for you to do is to turn in." He grinned. "You can go enjoy your birthday present."

One of the gifts the guys had given him was a couple of porn flicks, and the master bedroom had a TV and a Blu-ray player.

Steele chuckled, then pushed away from the counter and headed up the stairs. Getting some sleep was a good idea. Then he'd get up tomorrow and just enjoy the sunshine and the beautiful lake beside the cabin. As he walked up the stairs, he slid his hand over the inside pocket of his jacket to feel the two Blu-rays there. But he could put off sleep for a little, just to relieve the tension.

                    ⁰   ⁰   ⁰

A sound jarred Laurie from the light, fitful sleep she'd fallen into and she clutched the big fluffy comforter closer around her with her unbound hand. She was covered from head to toe, peering out from inside the cocoon.

Was the biker coming back to take her?

The door opened and the light flicked on. In the doorway stood an even bigger, tougher-looking biker. He didn't even glance her way, just closed the door behind him and stripped off his black leather jacket. He pulled something out of the pocket and tossed the garment on the dresser, then opened the doors of the armoire at the end of the bed to reveal a big TV. He turned it on, then put a disc into the player below it.

Images of naked people appeared on the screen. It was obviously lead-in credits for a porn film. He watched for a few moments, then pulled his T-shirt over his head, revealing bulging muscles and a snake tattoo coiling around his bicep then across his chest. Her heart raced as he unzipped his jeans and dropped them to the floor, then stepped out of them.

She held her breath when she saw him hook his thumbs in the elastic of his boxers, then push them down. Oh, God, he was going to get into bed with her and . . . He was going to force her to—

Her breath caught when he stood up.

God, she'd never seen a cock that big. She'd never even *imagined* a cock that big. Even though it was just starting to swell with need, it was gigantic. And frightening. Impressive. And intimidating.

He turned toward the bed and she sucked in a breath.

His eyes narrowed as his gaze jerked to her.

"What the hell?" He grabbed the covers and tossed them back, ripping away her only protection.

Steele stared at the woman lying in his bed. The sight of her long, shapely legs and slim, but curvy body sent blood straight to his groin. She shifted back and a chain clinked. That's when he realized one of her wrists was handcuffed to the headboard.

Fuck, this was why Shock had suggested he turn in. Not to watch porn, but to enjoy the birthday present awaiting him in his bed!

He smiled. "Well, hello there."

Should he slide his cock in her sweet, luscious mouth first, or glide into her hot, melting pussy?

What the fuck? She was here for the night. He could fuck her right now, relieving his ache, then have her revive him with a blow job and start all over again.

He chuckled and climbed into bed beside her, then shifted closer. He reached for her hand to pull it to his cock, wanting to feel her soft feminine fingers wrapped around him, but as soon as he touched her, she jerked away.

"No, please . . ." Panic flashed in her wide, blue eyes and she was practically panting in fear.

"What the fuck?"

Then he saw the sparkle of diamonds around her neck. It was the choker Craig's sister had received as a gift from her boyfriend at the bar earlier that night.

What the hell was going on here? Steele rolled away from her and sat up, placing his feet on the floor. He stared at the frightened woman, who was sucking in air, panic showing in her widened eyes.

He raked his hand through his hair. "How the hell did you get here?"

Someone started pounding on his door.

"Steele, it's Wild Card."

Then the door swung open and Wild Card burst inside. "I fell asleep on the couch. I didn't mean to . . ."

His gaze fell on Steele's naked form, then darted to the woman in the bed. Then he shook his head, holding up his hands, palms toward Steele, in a defensive gesture. "Steele, you gotta listen to me."

Anger surged through Steele and he lurched to his feet. "Wild Card, what the fuck did you do?"

"I didn't mean to—"

Steele strode toward him. "How the hell did you miss the fact that the plan was *not* to kidnap the woman?"

Laurie lay in the bed trembling as testosterone rippled through the room. She barely heard as the one called Wild Card—her kidnapper—explained to the man who was obviously the leader about how Donovan had treated her.

"The asshole was going to hurt her. I couldn't let him do that."

The man named Steele frowned.

Despite her shock and fear, she couldn't help staring at him in awe. His was stunningly handsome, with a square jaw and classic sculpted features that were totally at odds with his biker image. He almost reminded her of James Bond.

"And then when he offered me money to have sex with her—" Wild Card shook his head. "I told you. The guy is a real asshole. I had to get her away from him. And I couldn't just take her home. An abusive guy like that is going to go after her. And he'll punish *her* for what I did."

Steele sucked in a deep breath, then glanced at her. She cringed as his granite gaze locked on her.

"Why do you have her handcuffed? She looks terrified."

"She didn't exactly come here willingly."

"Fuck. So you really did kidnap her."

"She had just been traumatized and wasn't really thinking straight. And she has reason not to trust anyone right now."

"So why my bed? And with handcuffs?"

Wild Card shrugged. "I had to handcuff her so she wouldn't take off. And I couldn't just put her in a room alone overnight. Not handcuffed. What if there was a fire or something? Or she needed something? I knew the only person you'd be happy to have watching over her overnight would be you. As much as you trust us, she's under your protection."

"God damn it, Wild Card. Why do you have to make so much fucking sense?"

Steele slumped on the bed and raked his hand through his hair. "Fine. Now get lost. I'm going to have to figure out what the hell we're going to do about this."

Wild Card walked to the door and then turned. "Happy birthday, Steele." Then he closed the door behind him.

"Yeah, happy fucking birthday to me," he grumbled.

He turned to her and she stiffened.

"My name's Steele. And you're Laurie. I'm a friend of your brother's."

The fact he knew her name told her they hadn't kidnapped her randomly. She'd been targeted for some reason. She remembered his earlier words about a plan. It sounded like they'd planned to kidnap her, then changed their minds.

"Look, I don't know who you are or why you're trying to get me to trust you, but that's not going to happen. All I want is for you to let me go."

"Your brother's name is Craig."

She narrowed her eyes. Were they after ransom? If so, they would have researched her family connections to know who to send the ransom request to.

"Look, if you're trying to get ransom from Craig, you need to understand that he doesn't have a lot of money."

"I know that. I'm not after ransom money."

If he had discovered Craig wasn't rich, that could be why they had rejected her as a victim.

But Donovan was a wealthy man and everyone knew it. Were they planning on approaching him for money?

Her blood turned cold. He would pay it. She wanted to be free of the man, but this would put her in his debt.

After the vicious way he'd treated her tonight, she actually wondered if he might have set this up as some sick kind of control thing. To make her totally aware of how much power he had over her. Maybe he would even show up and play out some scenarios his sick mind might entertain. Like watching these bikers gangbang her, just like he'd suggested in the parking garage.

Her mind was raging with wild notions, and maybe that's all they were. All she knew for sure was she couldn't trust anything these men told her.

The big man beside her sighed deeply. "I see I'm not going to get anywhere with this tonight."

He leaned toward her and she cringed away, but he simply grabbed the covers and pulled them over her, then lay back in bed.

"I'm going to sleep. I suggest you do the same."

Steele rolled over and turned out the light.

Not that he fell asleep soon. He could sense the woman quivering on the other side of the bed. He wanted to console her and assure her everything would be all right, but there was nothing he could do right now that would make her trust him. Trust was only achieved by actions, and the only actions by him and his man Wild Card was to be torn away from her friends and family and brought to this isolated cabin. And her bad-news boyfriend, but that only made it worse. Being taken from one situation where she was totally helpless, to another, didn't inspire confidence.

In the morning, he'd sort this out somehow. He could roll over right now and promise he'd take her home tomorrow, but he was a man of his word and had learned better than to make promises until he knew the whole situation and what the consequences would be. Wild Card had kidnapped her. She could lay charges and have them all arrested. He'd like to contact Killer, and her brother, to see if they could sort this out without that kind of complication. Also, he didn't want to just return her to a situation where she would be in danger from her boyfriend. Hopefully, she was smart enough to consider him her ex-boyfriend by now, because the things Wild Card told him the guy had said and done tonight showed that he would have no qualms about brutalizing her. And the man obviously had means, so that meant he'd be more likely to get away with it.

What a fucking lousy way to end his birthday.

Steele opened his eyes and glanced around. A warm, female body was snuggled up against him, his arm around her. Her chestnut hair tickled his nose and he breathed in the sweet scent of it. Lily of the Valley. He lay still, enjoying the sensation of her soft, feminine curves pressed tight to him.

Maybe too much, because his cock began to swell.

She murmured in her sleep and shifted against him, her hand gliding along his torso. It brushed his cock, which was now semierect. At the feel of her hand brushing against it, it jerked to full attention.

He knew the instant she woke up. Her whole body stiffened. Then her hand jerked away from his member and her eyelids popped open. She stared at him with accusing blue eyes. Big, beautiful blue eyes with a dark rim around the pupil, and a scattering of golden specs, which probably glittered like sparks when she was angry.

She pushed herself away from him and skittered backward to the edge of the bed. The clank of the chain reminded him she was still handcuffed to the headboard.

"Good morning," he said, but she merely glared at him.

He sighed and sat up, then pushed back the covers. He was sure the sight of his big hard-on did not inspire confidence in her, but there was nothing he could do about that. It was what it was.

He stood up and walked to the private bathroom connected to the room and took a quick shower, conscious of leaving the woman alone and handcuffed to the bed. He returned and grabbed clean underwear from his drawer and pulled them on, then retrieved his jeans. Wild Card had left the key to the handcuffs on the dresser, so he picked it up and approached the bed.

When she saw him coming, she cowered under the covers.

"You slept in my bed last night, me naked, and I didn't touch you. Why do you think I would now?"

Laurie watched him warily as he wrapped his big hand around her wrist and unlocked the cuff around it.

"Because you were tired last night?" she suggested as she rubbed the red mark around her wrist.

He chuckled. "Sweetheart, I'm never too tired to fuck."

His words sent a tremor through her. She believed him. And the fact that he hadn't touched her made her feel that she wasn't in danger that way from him.

"There's a bathroom right there. You can shower and whatever. And just in case you're going to try something foolish like climbing out the window, I'll have someone watching from outside." He smiled. "I wouldn't want you to hurt yourself falling from the second story."

The room they were in was rustic, the walls showing the raw logs that made up the structure. The heavy wood furnishings matched the color and feel of the logs. It was very much a man's room, sparse and functional, but with a comforting appeal, Modern amenities, such as a large, flat-screen TV and Blu-ray player, blended into the décor in an artistic balance of clean lines and rough-hewn furnishings. The bed was big and comfortable with a cushioned bench at the foot, and a big, cozy armchair stood off to the side.

The whole house probably had the same outdoorsy male feel.

She stood up, tugging on the hem of the stupid short dress.

"I just have to ask," he said as he watched her with a grin. "Why wear a dress like that if you're so uncomfortable in it?"

She pursed her lips. She didn't want to admit to him that she'd worn it because Donovan had insisted. She still didn't understand why she had fallen into line with Donovan's controlling demands. What did that say about her as a strong, independent woman? How had she let that happen?

So she ignored his question and marched to the bathroom, closing the door behind her. The doorknob was black wrought iron, and the door closed with a satisfying thunk. She turned the lock.

It was steamy in the room, and smelled all musky and masculine. It must be the soap Steele used because it smelled just like him.

She glanced around at the surprisingly large bathroom, with a big, deep, old-fashioned soaker tub, a large glassed-in shower stall along the end wall, and a window overlooking the lake on one side and the dense trees surrounding the cabin on the other. She could easily pull open the window and climb out, but Steele had cautioned her he would have people watching. She frowned. She didn't relish climbing down from the second story anyway and she definitely wouldn't get far barefoot.

A fluffy white bath towel was folded neatly on a shelf over the toilet. Another one was thrown haphazardly over the edge of the tub, still damp, probably the one Steele had used to dry off his big, muscular, *naked* body.

The scent of him filled her nostrils, and the memory of waking up snuggled close to the big man, his arm around her, jolted through her. At first, she had felt warm and protected. Then she'd realized her wrist was pressed against his hard, hot cock and she'd jerked away.

But that initial feeling . . . that feeling deep in her

gut . . . that she was safe in his arms . . . That really threw her.

It was probably because she was looking for a safe haven in a storm. Steele wasn't the one who'd kidnapped her. And he hadn't touched her last night, even though he'd assured her this morning, he was *never too tired to fuck*.

But she couldn't trust him. Any more than she could trust Donovan.

Everything that had happened last night suddenly hit her full throttle. Even before the crazy biker had kidnapped her. The way Donovan had treated her. If Wild Card hadn't shown up when he had, Donovan would have taken her against that post. Against her will.

She sank to the floor, curling into a ball on the large, fluffy mat that filled the center of the room as her throat closed up. He would have *raped* her.

Tears flooded her eyes as she realized she had let herself get sucked into an abusive relationship. One where she had given up control to a ruthless, violent man.

How had she let that happen?

Oh, God, she'd been an idiot. Craig had cautioned her to be wary of Donovan, but he was her brother . . . and an overprotective one at that. She hadn't heeded his warnings. She'd been so headstrong and sure of herself. And Donovan had been so charming . . . at first.

He'd known exactly how to gain her confidence. And how to keep her under his thumb. She'd graduated from university five years ago with a communications degree, but with the job market the way it was, all she'd been able to get were service jobs. She'd been a barista for a while, then moved on to retail, but it was part-time work with lousy schedules. And lousy pay.

Once she and Donovan started dating, Donovan had gotten her a job in the local office of one of his companies working in the marketing department. The job gave her the stability she so craved and the income to finally buy her own home. Donovan had even arranged a great deal on a brand-new town house for her.

When he'd started controlling her, she'd turned a blind eye. Deep inside, she worried that if she broke up with him, it could put her job in danger, and without the job, she couldn't afford her mortgage.

He'd started with mild demands at first, then bigger ones. He'd cajoled her into letting him command her in the bedroom, even binding her sometimes. At first it had been sexy, submitting to a strong, dominating man, but he didn't always satisfy her, and had started doing things she wasn't really comfortable with.

Then when he'd wrapped his hands around her throat and choked her while he took his pleasure, she had realized she had to get out. Never would she have believed he would be capable of the things he'd said and done in the parking garage.

She realized she was trembling all over and a sob escaped her throat. She hugged her knees tighter to her body as she gave herself over to blind emotion, allowing the tears to flow.

A sharp knocking sounded at the door. "You all right in there?" Steele said through the door.

"Don't come in," she pleaded. The door was locked,

but she didn't for a minute think that he couldn't get in here if he wanted. And she didn't want him to see her like this. Whimpering and vulnerable. She scrambled to her feet.

"I won't. Just take your shower, then I'll get you something to eat."

"Okay," she said, and listened for the sound of his footsteps as he walked away from the door. Once she was sure he was gone, she stripped off her clothes quickly and stepped into the shower stall. The musky scent of Steele was even stronger in the small space and she breathed it in as she turned on the water.

In spite of herself, she found something about his scent deeply comforting. She let out a breath, breathed him in again, and felt her muscles begin to relax. She soaped her body and scrubbed hard.

She knew her response to Steele was stupid, that she was just looking for someone to watch over her, and he was a big, strong, powerful leader, a perfect man to protect her. But she needed to do that for herself. Depending on anyone else was a mistake she didn't intend to make again.

She washed her hair, then rinsed herself off and stepped from the stall. She grabbed the clean towel over the toilet and vigorously rubbed her hair. She dried her body, too, then slipped on her panties and bra. Her gaze fell to the tiny black dress lying on the floor. She did not want to put that thing back on.

She grabbed the big towel that Steele must have used after his shower and wrapped it around herself. It covered way more of her than the dress did.

Maybe she could ask Steele for some other clothes. One of his shirts. His jeans would be too big, but maybe he'd have something. Anything would be better than that revealing, skintight dress.

She turned the lock and opened the door, then stepped into the bedroom.

Steele glanced up as the bathroom door opened. He wasn't prepared for the sight of her all wrapped up in a towel, her hair damp and falling loosely over her shoulders. Unlike the polished party girl she'd seemed in the little black dress, now she looked all soft and vulnerable.

And sexy.

He couldn't help thinking about the fact she was naked under that towel.

He couldn't help thinking about unwrapping that towel to reveal her soft, round breasts.

"I . . . uh . . . wanted to know if you had something I could wear."

His eyebrow arched. "You don't like your dress?"

As soon as his gaze settled on her face, and her red puffy eyes, he realized she'd been crying. Protective urges raced through him. He wanted to fold her in his arms and hold her. To assure her everything would be all right.

"It's a little dressy for the whole kidnappee-hanging-around-the-log-cabin scenario, don't you think?" she said lightly.

His gaze shifted to the glint of diamonds around her neck.

"True. But I think the necklace trumps the dress."

Her hand flew to her neck. "Damn." She reached around behind her neck, but her towel slipped and she grabbed it.

Clearly, she wanted the choker off.

"Here, let me." He walked behind her and stroked her hair to the side, then worked at the catch on the diamond necklace.

The feel of his warm fingers brushing against her skin as he unfastened the choker sent shivers down Laurie's spine. His touch was gentle and somehow reassuring.

The necklace dropped away from her neck and she drew in a deep breath. It was like finally being free of Donovan.

Steele slid the necklace from her skin, then walked in front of her again. Then he held the very expensive necklace out to her. She took the delicate piece from his big fingers, not quite sure what to do with it. She wanted to throw it out the window, to totally reject the unwanted reminder of Donovan, but she couldn't do that.

The fact that Steele gave her back the expensive piece of jewelry reassured her somehow. If he wanted money, that thing was probably worth a lot. Of course, the gesture was just symbolic, because as long as he held her captive he could take it from her at any time. He could just be giving her a false sense of security.

But her gut said otherwise.

"I put a change of clothes on the bed for you. Hopefully they're more to your liking."

She walked toward the bed where a T-shirt and jeans sat neatly folded. She picked up the black shirt and glanced at it. It was adorned with hearts and skulls and a smattering of glitter, and was far too small to fit the big biker's broad chest.

"Where did you get women's clothes?" she asked.

"Those are Raven's. She rides with us. I thought you'd like a change of clothes and she was happy to help."

"Oh, well, please tell her thank you."

He nodded. "I'm going downstairs. Join us when you're dressed."

She watched him cross the room and go out the door. As soon as the door closed behind him, she dropped the towel and tugged the shirt over her head. Then she pulled on the jeans. They were well worn, with shredded bare spots on the legs, and were a little loose around the waist, but there was a studded, black leather belt on the bed, so she pulled that through the loops and tightened it.

She glanced in the mirror at herself. Add black leather wristbands and a leather jacket and she'd pass for a biker chick.

This Raven woman *was* a biker chick, which meant she was one of the gang. Any hopes of gaining her sympathies and maybe talking her into helping Laurie escape evaporated.

She sat on the bed and wondered what to do next. If she just stayed up here, Steele was bound to come and get her. Maybe at that point his patient manner would change, just like Donovan's charming manner had changed when he became annoyed with her. She didn't want to chance it.

Anyway, she could use a cup of coffee, and she was getting hungry.

She walked to the door and grasped the heavy black doorknob, then turned it, her heart thumping loudly. She peered out the door and saw no one in the long, wide hallway. She slipped from the room and closed the door, then walked along the hardwood floor toward the stairs. She could hear masculine voices talking downstairs.

"There you are," an unfamiliar male voice said behind her, then strong arms wrapped around her waist and she sucked in a breath as she was tugged through a doorway and spun around.

Untamed

Laurie's hair swirled in her face and she found herself encased in big strong arms, and a raspy masculine face brushed her cheek as the man's mouth found hers through the curtain of hair. His tongue teased her lips but she turned her face away as she pushed against his chest.

"Baby, what's wrong?" he asked as he loosened his hold, but didn't let her go. Then he pushed back the hair covering her face. "Oh, shit."

"'Oh, shit' is right," a woman said from behind her. "What are you doing, Rip?"

The man named Rip released Laurie and she scurried back, then he glanced at the woman in the doorway. She simply stared at him with an amused smile.

"Raven, I thought it was you. Those *are* your jeans with the rhinestones on the pockets."

Raven pushed herself from the doorway and stepped forward.

"Because my ass looks like any other woman's in those jeans." She circled around behind Laurie. Then she smiled.

"Okay, if you think my ass is as great as that, you're forgiven." She stepped into Rip's arms and kissed him, then he pulled her tighter and deepened the kiss.

Laurie just stood frozen to the spot. She was still trembling from being dragged into the bedroom with yet another rough biker. The fact that it had been a case of mistaken identity didn't alleviate the rush of adrenaline through her.

Finally, the couple parted and the woman gazed at her, then stuck out her hand.

"Hi, I'm Raven."

Laurie took the offered hand and shook it.

Raven nudged the man beside her, who had slipped his arm around her waist. "And this crazy man is Rip."

Rip held out his hand, but Laurie couldn't bring herself to take it. He drew it back.

"Sorry about the kiss. I didn't mean to scare you," he said.

Laurie pushed her shoulders back. "I wasn't scared."

Raven grinned. "You're probably hungry. Shock makes a mean omelet and I smell bacon. Why don't you go ahead down? We'll be along later."

Laurie nodded, then left the room. As she walked down the hall, they closed the door and from the way they'd looked at each other, she had no doubt about what the couple would be doing in there.

They didn't seem to be worried about her escaping, but why should they, knowing others were downstairs.

She started along the dark-stained oak hardwood

floor toward the stairs again, her heart thumping. It had been dark when Wild Card had brought her in last night, but she remembered that on the main floor the stairway was a short straight path from the door. She took the first few steps down the solid wood stairs. She could see the entryway and the front door ahead. The stairway was wide, but closed on either side.

She clung to the smooth, wall-mounted wood railing as she continued. As she approached the bottom, she peered around. There was a large room with big sunny windows to the left and a small hall with a couple of doorways on the right. She could smell bacon from that direction.

Maybe the others were in the kitchen eating.

As quietly as she could, she hurried toward the door, then reached for the knob.

"Don't even think about it."

Steele's commanding voice stopped her in her tracks. She couldn't see him, but his voice came from the big, bright room on her left.

"Come in here and sit down," he said.

Defeated, she turned away from her possible escape.

Wild Card, the man who had kidnapped her last night and brought her here, came out of the room and walked toward her. He wasn't as tall as Steele, but he was still intimidating, towering over her. She still remembered leaning against his big, hard chest, his arm around her waist as they had sped through the night on his motorcycle. And how frightened she'd been.

And still was.

She drew in a breath.

"You okay?" His hazel eyes were warm and concerned.

She shook her head. "I've been kidnapped and brought here against my will, and I'm being held captive." She stared up at him with as much defiance as she could muster. "So, to answer your question, no, I'm not all right."

Instead of looking apologetic, he simply held her gaze. "I know you don't like the situation you're in, but I'm not sorry about bringing you here. Have you thought about what would have happened if I hadn't come along and gotten you away from that asshole?"

A shiver shuddered through her.

"That guy was going to hurt you," he continued, "and you know that. I couldn't let that happen."

He gestured toward the other room and she walked toward it.

As soon as she stepped into the big room, filled with sunshine from the huge windows overlooking a glittering lake, she was aware of Steele. He sat in a big armchair, his booted foot resting on the wooden coffee table with wrought-iron trim in front of him as he stared outside, sipping from a steaming mug.

The blended décor continued through the rest of the house, with the log walls and heavy wooden cabinets and shelves, and the latest electronics tucked into place in the rustic furniture. The upholstered furniture was big and comfortable looking, in earth tones.

"You can sit at the table. Shock is making you some breakfast," Wild Card said as he followed her.

Laurie walked to the dining table at the far end of the room and sat down.

"Coffee?" Wild Card picked up a thermal jug and poured steaming coffee into one of several empty mugs sitting on the table.

Laurie nodded, her throat too choked up from memories of last night and the way Donovan had treated her. And the realization that if this man hadn't shown up, Donovan would have hurt her. If he'd stopped even pretending to be civilized, she was sure he was capable of raping her, beating her . . . hurting her badly. And with his money, he would make any potential consequences just go away.

Wild Card pushed the filled mug toward her, then poured another. Laurie poured cream into her cup, then added a spoonful of sugar and stirred. As she lifted the cup, the aroma helped draw her from her dark thoughts. When she took a sip, her taste buds danced at the delightful flavor.

Wild Card smiled. "Yeah, the people who own this place have great taste in coffee."

Her gaze darted to his. "Did you break into this house?"

"No," Steele said. "A friend arranged for us to stay here."

A few minutes later, another tattooed man came into the room with a plate of food. He had the darkest brown eyes she'd ever seen, with an even darker rim around the edges. His hair was thick and wavy, long on top and cut tight at the sides, accentuating his ruggedly handsome face. On his bicep was a bright-colored star tattoo. As he walked closer, she realized that there were two dragons—one red, one blue—framed in the star, facing each other, each with a claw on a single sphere between them.

. He walked toward the table and smiled.

"Hi. My name's Shock." He placed the plate in front of her. "I hope you like western omelets."

She glanced at the perfect half-moon-shaped omelet with two strips of bacon lying beside it and a sprig of parsley. It smelled heavenly. Who knew a rough-and-tumble, badass biker could cook. And with such a flourish.

She nodded. "Thank you."

Shock poured himself a cup of coffee and sat beside Steele.

Laurie ate in silence. She could only manage half of the omelet and didn't even touch the bacon, before she pushed away the plate. She glanced at Steele, still taken aback at his stunning good looks. Her gaze shifted to Shock then to Wild Card, who sat across the table from her. He watched her but didn't say anything.

She drew in a deep breath. "So what happens now?"

Wild Card pulled her plate toward him and grabbed a strip of bacon. "Well, since Shock cooked, I guess I'll be doing dishes."

She pursed her lips. "How long are you going to keep me here?"

"That's a good question," Steele said. "One I don't have an answer for."

Her stomach tightened. What did they want from her? The sound of footsteps hurrying down the stairway and a woman laughing interrupted the flow of questions swirling through her brain. Raven burst around the corner followed by Rip. He grabbed her arm and pulled her back to him, then drew her into a deep kiss. She wore an oversized T-shirt and nothing else and when his arm tightened around her waist, the hem of the garment hiked up and Laurie assumed they'd all get a good view of lacy undies, or maybe bare flesh if Raven was wearing a thong, but the flash of red fabric under the shirt covered the essentials.

"I'm going into town to pick up the list of groceries Shock asked for," Rip said. "Anyone else want anything?"

"If cream's not on the list, add it," Steele said.

"And more beer," Shock added.

"Cream and beer. You got it." Rip kissed Raven again. "You be good."

Raven grinned. "Oh, I'll be better than good. I'll be exceptional." She glanced at the men in the living room. "Right guys?"

"She's always been exceptional when I've been with her," Shock said with a grin.

"Me, too," said Wild Card.

Rip chuckled then kissed her again. "I'll see you when I get back." He strode to the door and went outside.

"I'm going for a swim." She smiled enticingly. "Anyone want to join me?"

"Not me," Wild Card said. "I'm on cleanup duty."

"And I'm resting up after slaving over a hot stove," said Shock.

"Steele?"

He shook his head. "Maybe later, Rave."

Her gaze slid to Laurie, but then flickered away. "Okay, you know where to find me."

She walked to a big cupboard by the window and pulled out a beach towel, then slipped out the front door. Laurie watched her through the big window facing the driveway as she trotted along a grassy path heading toward bushes, instead of toward the beach they could see from the window facing the lake.

Wild Card picked up Laurie's plate and the two empty mugs, then headed out of the room. Long moments passed and no one said anything.

Laurie sat impatiently, wondering what to do next. The two men seemed happy to just ignore her. Shock had picked up a book and was reading while Steele just gazed outside.

She stood up and walked across the room, having to pass behind the men sitting on the couch.

"What are you doing?" Steele asked.

"Nothing."

She kept moving toward the front of the house. He stood up and followed her. Her heart thumped, but she walked toward the entrance, and the front door.

She reached for the doorknob.

"Where are you going?"

She gripped it and hesitated. "Nowhere."

He said nothing more, so she turned the knob.

"You said you weren't going anywhere."

She glanced at him. "I just want to go outside."

"No."

"But I—"

"No." His tone was sharp this time.

She drew in a deep breath and sighed. "You're treating me like a child."

His lips turned up in a grin, wiping away the severe expression of a moment ago. "Maybe I should spank your bottom."

She drew in a deep breath as she stared at him. The thought of his big hand smacking across her bare behind sent a shudder through her that wasn't entirely unpleasant. A confusion of need and anxiety swirled through her. She didn't know what to make of her own response.

His expression turned serious again. "Don't look at me like that. I'm not really going to punish you."

Her throat tightened and she dropped her gaze to the floor, then stepped back from the door.

Damn, the trapped frightened look in her eyes tore at Steele's heart. Clearly, she didn't believe him. And why should she? They had brought her here against her will, and now they wouldn't let her go. She had no reason to trust him. And given how her boyfriend had treated her in the parking garage, she had no reason to trust any man.

A question sprang to his mind. Had that bastard of a boyfriend mistreated her before? And how badly?

"Laurie, I'm not going to hurt you. I promise you that. Nor will anyone else here. You're under my protection."

She nodded again. "I just . . . want to go outside," she said in a stilted voice. "I need fresh air. And exercise." She drew in a deep breath, her hands clenched at her sides. "I just want to go for a walk."

He grinned. "Now you sound like a dog."

"Does that mean you're going to put me on a leash?" she asked, her eyes flashing.

He almost thought she was joking to lighten the mood, but the haunted look in her eyes told him maybe she was talking from experience . . . and not a pleasant one.

He gazed at her, assessing. It wasn't right to keep her locked up in here. The sun was shining outside. It was a beautiful summer day, meant to be enjoyed in such a stunning location.

Wild Card appeared from the kitchen and walked toward them. "Why don't I go for a walk with her?"

Steele glanced at her, wondering how she'd feel about that since Wild Card was the one who had kidnapped her, but her expression gave nothing away. Well, that was the choice she was given. Go with Wild Card, or stay here.

"Okay, but under one condition." He was not going to chance her running off. He could tell she was just as headstrong as his sister Chrissy had been, and would defy him just for the sake of it, so until he could convince her she was better off staying here, he had to take every precaution to protect her.

Laurie's stomach tensed as the door swung open, revealing the gravel road leading to the cabin. The damned man had handcuffed her to Wild Card, which had dashed her hopes of finding a way to slip free and disappear down that path.

She stepped outside, Wild Card by her side. She breathed in the fresh air, enjoying the sunshine on her face and naked arms. There were three big motorcycles parked in the gravel area by the house. The man named Rip had gone into town, so there was one bike for each man in the house, but not one for Raven.

If Laurie could figure out how to drive one of the big machines, maybe at some point she could use one to escape, but even if she could slip away from her escort, they would hear her start it up, and they would be able to easily chase her down. Either way, she'd probably be killed trying to ride one of those things any distance. And she didn't even know how to start one, or even if they needed a key like a car.

"The place where Raven went to swim is over that way." Wild Card pointed to a path that disappeared through the trees as he fell into step beside her. "There's a beach out in front of the cabin, but she found a quiet, secluded spot she likes. She's probably still swimming if you want to join her."

"What about these?" she asked, hoping he'd suggest taking them off.

He shrugged. "They can get wet."

Disappointment washed through her, but she would dearly love to go for a swim on this beautiful day. She loved the water.

"I don't have a bathing suit," she said.

He grinned. "That never stopped Raven."

Laurie stiffened.

"Oh, no, look . . . I wasn't suggesting anything. Like Steele said, no one here's going to hurt you in any way. I just meant you could swim in your . . . uh . . ." Finally, he just shook his head. "Never mind."

She held her silence as they walked along the grass.

He sighed. "I really am sorry you're stuck here when you don't want to be."

She nodded. "You've already explained that."

She didn't want to hear him tell her again that he'd done it for her own good. She didn't want to think about the fact she had a boyfriend who wanted to hurt her. And she didn't want to think about the fact when she went back, he would find her and make her pay for embarrassing him. And defying him.

A cell phone rang and Wild Card pulled it from his pocket. "Yeah?" He glanced toward the house. "Okay, I'll go find him and call you back." He glanced at Laurie as he slipped the phone back into his pocket. "We have to go back in the house."

She gazed at him with pleading eyes. "No, please, just a little longer."

"I have to find Steele."

"Just let me stay out here until you get back." She glanced around and pointed to a deck along one side of the house with a hot tub. "You could handcuff me to the railing."

He glanced at the wooden railing and gazed at her, then reached in his back pocket.

"Okay." He led her to the deck, which was only a few

steps up and unlocked his cuff and fastened it around the first post at the bottom of the stairs.

"I'll be right back."

He shoved the key in his back pocket, but as he walked away, she noticed that it had actually fallen to the ground. It landed on the grass, so it made no sound.

Wild Card disappeared into the house. She stood frozen for a moment, overjoyed at her good luck. She had intended to try and find a way to break the post, or kick it from the railing and pull the cuff free, which was a long shot, but now she didn't have to.

She leaned over and tried to reach the key, but it was a little too far away. She stretched out her leg and was able to pull it closer, then pick it up and unlock the cuff.

She sucked in a deep breath, thrilled at her newfound freedom, then hurried toward the path leading to the bushes. Wild Card had said that Raven was swimming in a secluded spot. They probably wouldn't expect her to go in that direction, since he'd told her Raven had gone this way, but even if they did, she hoped she could slip past where the woman was swimming and disappear into the woods.

She didn't relish fighting her way through the brush, wild animals possibly about, but she knew if she stayed to the road, they would find her right away.

Her heart hammered as she approached the bushes, then sighed in relief as she stepped out of sight of the cabin. The path was merely a balding strip through the grass, worn down by people continually treading on it.

The trees weren't very dense so she easily made her way along the path. She headed toward thicker brush ahead, feeling far too visible here. She needed to be out of sight, and she needed somewhere to hide once they found out she was missing.

Once she reached the bushes, rather than relaxing, her heart pounded faster. She was really doing this. Trying to escape the big, tough bikers who had kidnapped her.

Soon she saw the glitter of water through the trees ahead. As she drew nearer, she saw a flash of red. When she looked closer, she realized it was a red bikini, abandoned on the small strip of sand at the water's edge. She looked out in the water and saw Raven sitting on a rock in the water, her bare breasts visible above the surface.

Oh, God, how could the woman just discard her bathing suit like that and expose herself with all these men around?

She drew in a deep breath and decided she should be able to slip by and continue through the woods without the woman seeing her, but as she continued along the path, Raven pushed herself from the rock and slipped into the water, which was only to her waist it turned out, then started walking toward the shore. Laurie scooted along the path faster, wanting to get past where Raven could see her before she reached the shore.

"Hey, bitch."

Laurie froze in her tracks. The male voice, which sent a shudder of dread through her, wasn't familiar. And it wasn't close to her. She ducked down, but kept moving closer to the lake, being careful to stay hidden. As she got closer, she saw a big man with short-cropped hair and a fringe of whiskers along his chin standing on the shore, wearing tight jeans and a black tank top that revealed his muscular shoulders and bulging arms, both covered in a tribal tattoo design.

Raven glanced at the tall, broad-shouldered man and her eyes narrowed.

"We've been looking for pussy," he said, as he un-zipped his pants.

We? Horrified, Laurie glanced around her, worried she'd see other bikers closing in on her. Were they from a rival gang?

Raven backed farther into the water, covering her naked breasts with her hands. But a man, who seemed to come from nowhere, stepped behind her and grabbed her arms.

"Oh, now, don't go covering those pretty breasts of yours."

The second man, who must have slipped into the water from the other side of the inlet, forced her arms behind her, thrusting her big breasts forward, the nipples puckered and hard.

He had waded into the water still in his jeans and T-shirt. The sleeves had been torn off, revealing arms just as bulging and inked as his friend's. His dark brown hair was cropped short on the sides and longer on the top, combed back from his face like a modern-day James Dean and look-ing every bit as untamed.

Laurie's heart pounded. A desperate need to escape her captivity still pulsed through her with every beat of her heart, but she couldn't leave Raven to these men. She needed to get help.

She turned and started to race back along the path. Adrenaline pumped through her and she panted as she flew as fast as she could. She pushed through the bushes, still only halfway back to the cabin, and wham! She slammed into a solid, masculine chest. Steele's arms came around her, stopping her from tumbling to the ground. She gasped and stared up at his angry face.

As she tried to catch her breath, she realized Wild Card was nowhere to be seen. She pointed toward the lake, but he grasped her shoulders, scowling.

"There you are. I didn't know where the hell you'd gone. What were you thinking running off like that?" His eyes flashed with anger. "From now on you don't get out of my sight. Mine or whoever I assign to watch you. Do you understand?"

Without thinking she nodded. "But—"

"No, buts. You would never have made it back on your own. Don't you know there are bears around here? And wolves."

"I mean . . . Raven . . ." She pointed to the lake. "She's in trouble."

"What?" A look of concern crossed Steele's face. "What kind of trouble?"

She grabbed his arm, her fingers curling around his solid, reassuring muscles, to pull him with her. He followed, pushing through the bushes with her.

"There are these two men." She had to run to keep up with his long-legged stride. "They're . . . um . . . assaulting her."

"Fuck." He drew his hand free and raced ahead of her. She ran as fast as she could to keep up, but he disappeared through the trees. She was just thankful that he would get to Raven quickly.

He would know what to do.

But when she caught up with him, he just stood by a large tree staring out over the water.

Laurie gazed at the sight of Raven, still standing naked in the water, one man only a foot in front of her and the other still holding her arms trapped behind her.

The man in front of her stepped closer. "Now suck my cock, bitch."

"And what if I don't want to?" Raven challenged.

The man behind her slid his arm around her waist and pulled her against his body, his muscular forearm brushing against the undersides of her naked breasts.

"No is not an acceptable answer." He pressed his hand to the top of her head and pushed her downward. She sank to her knees in front of the other man who then pressed his cock to her lips.

To Laurie's total surprise, Raven wrapped her hand around the big erection and opened her mouth, then took it inside.

"Aren't you going to do something?" Laurie murmured to Steele.

"I am. I'm watching."

Shock vaulted through her. She hadn't known Steele

very long, and even though he'd kidnapped her, or at least, his man Wild Card had, she'd felt he was honorable and protective of his people.

Yet here he was, simply watching while these two men forced Raven to pleasure them.

Raven glided her lips up and down the man's big member while the man behind her cupped her breast and stroked.

The man whose cock was in her mouth groaned. "Oh, fuck, Rave. Suck it."

Then he threw his head back and groaned his release. Raven drew back and licked her lips then stood up and turned to the other man.

Laurie's jaw dropped as she realized Raven knew these men.

"Now that I'm finished with Dom, where's that delicious cock of yours, Magic?" Raven asked, a salacious smile on her face.

"Right here and waiting for your talented mouth, love."

"Ah, you sweet talker." She started to sink to her knees again, but he tugged her into his arms and kissed her with passion.

When he released her, she laughed and sank down in front of him, then grasped his rigid cock and stroked it.

"She's cheating on Rip?" Laurie finally asked when she found her voice.

Steele shrugged. "It's not really cheating. There's an understanding."

"An understanding?" she echoed.

"Raven is Rip's woman. But he shares her with us."

Yet again, shock gripped Laurie at the realization that Raven was shared among all of the men in Steele's gang, despite the fact she was Rip's girlfriend.

Laurie couldn't tear her gaze from the erotic scene unfolding in the water in front of her. She knew she should walk away. Just go back to the cabin right now. She shouldn't be watching such an intimate scene between the three people, but she couldn't seem to move.

She was very conscious of Steele standing behind her. So big and masculine.

After a moment, his hand wrapped around her waist and he drew her back against his solid body.

Oh, God, she was so turned on watching Raven's mouth gliding along the man's big, hard cock. And knowing the other man had just climaxed in her mouth.

As Laurie watched Raven sucking on the thick shaft with exuberance, she suddenly found herself longing for the touch of a man.

"It's fucking hot watching them, isn't it?" Steele murmured against her ear, his breath causing wisps of hair to flutter across her cheek.

She sucked in a breath, startled at the reminder he was standing behind her. Not that she had actually forgotten. How could she, with him so close, and oozing such a strong masculine presence? But she had been trying to ignore it.

She was sure if she turned around and gave him any sign of willingness, he would kiss her. Then he would probably shove her up against the big tree behind them and take her.

Her insides ached at the thought. Right here, right now, she wanted him to. Oh, God, the craving was so intense she could barely stop herself from begging him to touch her.

As if sensing her thoughts, his hand skimmed under her breast.

She gasped, stiffening. She could feel his big erection pressing hard against her behind, only the layers of fabric between his aroused cock and her naked behind. His arm tightened around her and she struggled against the tight band of hard muscle.

His hand slid away from her breast, but he guided her to the big tree trunk and pressed her back against it. "I know you're turned on. And so am I."

His mouth found hers and he kissed her with fiery passion. His tongue teased her lips and then pushed inside, thoroughly exploring the inside of her mouth, forcing her lips wide. The thunder of the blood pumping through her veins pounded in her ears. The invasion of his tongue excited her.

She wanted to give in to him, to let him take her.

But she couldn't.

She pulled her mouth free. "No." The word came out on a breath of air, her voice filled with panic.

His dark eyes bored through her, assessing. His hand skimmed down her side and for a moment, she thought he intended to take her against the tree after all.

"I won't do anything you don't want me to do. But right now, I need to fuck someone."

His words confused her. He had her pushed up against the tree, his solid body trapping her against the rough bark, his hard cock pressed tight to her belly, making her knees go weak, yet he said he wouldn't do anything she didn't want.

Did he think she wanted this?

Oh, God, does it show so clearly in my eyes?

She shook her head. "Steele, please. I—"

But he stepped back, his blazing eyes pinning her to the spot. He pulled handcuffs out of his pocket and slapped a cuff on her wrist, then attached it to a thick, low-hanging branch.

"What are you doing?" she protested, her heart pounding.

"I know I said I wouldn't let you out of my sight, but right now I fucking need you to stay right here. Do you understand?"

At his commanding tone, she nodded.

He leaned in closer. "And if you find a way to run off this time, I swear to you, I will find you, and I won't be happy."

At his words, a tremor shuddered through her.

"Is that clear?"

She nodded, her stomach tight.

Then she watched as he turned around and headed toward the water, stripping off his T-shirt as he walked.

His torso was sublime, with hard muscles rippling

across his broad, sculpted back. A snake tattoo coiled around his bicep then across his chest. As he approached the water, he dropped his jeans and boxers onto the ground, then waded into the water.

Dom was perched on the big rock in the water, Raven sitting between his knees facing away from him as Magic's cock pushed into her slick opening in a slow, steady thrust.

"Fuck, Steele," Dom said, staring at Steele walking toward them. "I never get tired of seeing that big monster of a cock you have. And it's all ready for us."

Steele stepped close to Magic, then turned around. Laurie's eyes popped as she saw the incredible size of Steele's erect cock. She'd never seen anything like it.

Dom reached out and wrapped his hand around Steele's cock, then began to pump him.

Laurie sucked in a breath. God, that was the hottest thing she had ever seen. Her breasts ached with the need to be touched, so she slid her hand under her top and glided her finger over her hard nipple.

Magic was thrusting into Raven faster and she began to moan.

Laurie couldn't help herself. She tweaked her nipple, then stroked the other one.

"Oh, God, yes." Raven gasped and arched against the man fucking her. "Ooooh . . ." Then she wailed, her face glowing in ecstasy.

Laurie pinched her nipple, aching for a big cock inside her, too.

Magic groaned, then pulled Raven tight. The two

stayed locked in their embrace for a moment, then Magic drew back and kissed her.

"You are one sexy fucking bitch." Magic smiled and tipped up her chin, then kissed her one more time before stepping back.

"I was looking for pussy this time," Dom said as he released Steele's giant rod, "but I'll defer to you, as always, Steele."

Dom and Raven stood up and Raven leaned over, offering her naked ass to the men.

"Thanks, Dom," Raven said. "I'm not quite ready to take Steele's big, sexy monster from the back yet."

Dom laughed as he stepped behind her and slid his cock into her, gliding a few strokes then pulling out. Laurie was confused about the seeming contradiction, but then Dom pressed his hard cock, glistening with Raven's slickness, to her ass and slowly pushed forward. Laurie watched with wide eyes as Dom's hard cock slowly disappeared into Raven.

Laurie's insides clenched. Donovan had forced her to have anal sex once, but he had been harsh, driving into her before she was ready. He used the act almost as a punishment.

She had tried it before and knew if it was done with consideration and care, it could be a delightful experience, but after Donovan's rough treatment of her, she would be forever wary of the act.

From the look on Raven's face, however, she was definitely experiencing delight.

Dom wrapped his arms around her waist and drew her tight against his body, then he turned and sat on the rock. His big hands glided up her body and cupped both her breasts.

"God, I love a woman's soft breasts," he said.

Magic chuckled. "And a man's hard cock."

"Which yours isn't right now." Dom smiled. "But I can fix that."

As they were talking, Steele stepped toward Raven. She wrapped her hand around Steele's cock and drew it to her mouth, then kissed the tip.

"You a little frustrated, Steele?" Raven's tongue swirled over his tip and he groaned. "With a hot woman in your bed last night and no way to release your urges?"

He grasped her head and pulled her toward him, skewering her mouth with his enormous member.

"But I do have a way to relieve it as long as you're around."

Raven's cheeks hollowed and Steele groaned again. Oh, God, it was so hot watching her. Laurie couldn't stop thinking about the fact that Dom's cock was still inside her ass. Raven wrapped her hand around Steele's cock and bobbed up and down a few times, then drew back.

"It's my pleasure, Steele."

"Fuck, and ours," Dom said, reaching for Magic's cock.

Magic stepped forward and Dom took the other's man's cock in his mouth, sucking with gusto. Laurie pinched her nipples at the erotic sight of the hard cock inside the muscular, tattooed biker's mouth.

As Dom sucked Magic's cock, Steele drew his cock from Raven's mouth. She leaned back against Dom's chest, cradled between his thick thighs, and widened her legs.

Laurie's gaze locked on Steele's cock, which looked ready to burst. She couldn't believe any of this was happening—the past twenty-four hours had been absolutely insane. All she knew was that she'd never been so turned on in her life. The ache between her thighs was excruciating. She pinched her nipple again, then unzipped her jeans and slid her hand inside. As the big, hard cock slid into Raven, Laurie slid a finger inside her own slick opening. Oh, God, she was so wet with need.

Steele thrust forward and Raven moaned.

"Fuck, you are always so hot and tight," Steele said. "I love fucking you, woman."

Laurie drove her finger inside herself, a little jealous that it was Raven that Steele was talking to and not her.

Steele drew back, then drove forward again.

Hormones raged through Laurie as she watched the scene in front of her. Steele's massive cock driving into Raven, Dom's hips pivoting up and down as his cock glided into Raven's ass, and the whole while, Magic's big cock sliding in and out of Dom's mouth.

Magic grabbed Dom's head, then groaned, jerking against his face. Dom sucked as Magic shuddered against him. Finally, Magic drew away, his wilted cock dropping from Dom's mouth.

Dom turned to Raven and nuzzled her ear as he and Steele both drove into her. Laurie's gaze locked on Steele's face, her fingers stroking over her clit as she watched him fill Raven again and again. The intensity and desire emanating from him filled her with an even greater need. To feel his hands on *her*. To feel him invade *her* body with that big, hard cock of his. To feel his arms around her.

Raven began to moan.

"Are you close, baby?" Steele asked.

"Oh, yes. I love both of you fucking me." Raven's breathless words sent Laurie's senses reeling. She wanted to be Raven. To feel what Raven was feeling.

She wanted to feel Steele driving into her.

Steele began to groan and Laurie's fingertip flickered over her clit, driving her pleasure higher.

Dom groaned, his body tensing as he released inside Raven's body. Steele kept pounding into her, then groaned and thrust deep.

Laurie's pleasure peaked, her finger quivering over her sensitive bud, then she gasped as an orgasm claimed her.

Moments later, her eyelids popped open with a start and she gazed around, realizing she was outside, standing against a tree where anyone could happen across her, while she was touching herself intimately.

She tugged her hand from her jeans—actually Raven's jeans—her cheeks hot. She straightened her clothing and gazed up to see Steele wading from the water. The other three seemed content to swim, but Steele pulled on his clothes and walked through the trees toward her.

His gaze perused her, clearly noting her rosy cheeks and her uncomfortable stance. Could he tell?

If he could, he didn't say anything about it.

"Let's go." He unlocked the handcuffs and took her elbow, then guided her back through the trees toward the house.

For a man who had just had sex, he seemed incredibly tense. He had a tight grip on her arm and he marched her through the woods and toward the cabin with unflinching focus. He opened the door and pressed her into the house, then up the stairs.

Toward the bedroom.

He opened the door and pushed her inside, then closed the door behind him.

At the alarm that flared through her, she reminded herself if he'd wanted to, he could have taken her against the tree only moments ago. But he hadn't. And even if that hadn't been so, he'd just had sex with Raven, so he wouldn't even be ready again so soon.

"Clearly, I can't trust that you won't take any opportunity to escape, so my only choice is to keep you locked up."

She turned to him. "But that's not your only choice. Why don't you just let me go?" She licked her lips, wondering if she could convince him. "I won't press charges if that's what you're worried about."

He scowled. "One, I don't believe that. And, two, it's not about what happens to us. The bigger issue is what your so-called boyfriend will do to you once you go back."

She shifted uncomfortably. "Even if that's true, you can't keep me here forever."

"No, but I can keep you here until your brother gets back into town."

Her eyebrows rose. "How do you know about my brother anyway?" A knot formed in the pit of her stomach.

"He's a friend of a friend," he said.

She frowned, not believing him. "Look, he doesn't have a lot of money."

But she knew Craig would do whatever he could to get her back. Even bankrupt his business if that's what it took.

"I told you last night, I'm not going after your brother for ransom."

The dark thought rocked through her again that they must realize if they wanted ransom, they could get it from Donovan. He'd pay it. Not because he cared about her, but because he wanted to control her. If he was approached for ransom, he would quietly pay it. Then once he had his hands on her, he would probably lock her in the dungeon he had in his basement and no one would be the wiser. He could do anything he wanted to her. For as long as he wanted.

She felt sick at the thought.

As much as Steele talked of not wanting her to wind up in Donovan's clutches, was he saying that just to gain her trust? Or if it was true, would the lure of money override that?

Steele scowled. "I don't want ransom. Fuck, you are a hard woman to convince."

With that, he turned around and stormed out the door, slamming it behind him.

Steele plodded up the stairs. The thought of lying beside the hot woman sharing his bed and not being able to do anything about the surge of need that rose in him every time he got close to her had kept him downstairs drinking with the guys far longer than he'd intended. The others had finally all staggered off to bed, leaving Steele nursing his drink alone. He'd finally tossed it back, knowing he had to head to bed eventually.

Now it was very late, and he was tired. Which was just as well. Hopefully, he'd fall into bed and go straight to sleep.

He pushed open the door. The room was dark, except for the dim light of the moon glowing in the window. He could see the rounded shape of the young woman lying in his bed, one arm extended over her head and attached to the bedpost by the handcuffs. He'd had Raven keep her company over dinner, then give her an oversized T-shirt to sleep in and handcuff her again.

He stripped off his jeans and T-shirt, then drew back the covers and slid in beside her. Her back was to him, and he closed his eyes, trying to ignore her soft, warm body so close by, but he couldn't. His cock swelled at the thought she wore only a thin T-shirt over her naked body. And she was only inches away from him.

He clenched his jaw and closed his eyes, willing sleep to come. He was tired. Exhausted, actually. He should be able to drift off easily.

But his cock had other ideas. He'd had more to drink than he should have, and maybe he wasn't thinking as clearly as he should be, but it seemed to him there'd be nothing wrong if he just drew her soft body close to his. He wouldn't *do* anything.

And she'd snuggled up to him last night.

He shifted toward her and wrapped his arm around her waist, then drew her close to him. She was warm and soft, and her hair smelled of wildflowers.

Laurie woke up the minute the door opened. She'd felt him climb into bed behind her. She'd lain very still, hoping he'd just go to sleep, and at first she thought he had, but then he'd moved toward her. His arm slid around her and drew her close.

She tried to keep her body relaxed, hoping he'd think she was asleep. Hoping he'd move away. But when he pulled her a little tighter, she could feel his cock hard against her back and she stiffened. She could smell alcohol on his breath and . . . oh, God, he was obviously turned on. Was he going to do something about it? Would he . . . force her?

"What are you going to do?" she asked, her voice quavering.

"Fuck, I'm not going to *do* anything," he responded, his speech a little slurred. "I keep telling you that. I don't know why you don't fucking believe me."

"Maybe because you're holding on to me and . . . well, you're clearly turned on."

He cursed under his breath. "Is that a crime? Being turned on?"

He rolled away and got out of the bed, then started pulling on his clothes. He strode to the door and grabbed the doorknob.

"Wait. Before you go . . ."

"What?" he asked impatiently.

"I . . . have to go to the bathroom."

He scowled, but he walked to the dresser and picked up the key to the handcuffs, then walked to the bed and released her wrist. She scooted from the bed and headed to the bathroom. When she returned, he cuffed her again. As he stepped away, she noticed that the cuff around her wrist hadn't closed as tightly as before.

As soon as the door closed behind him, she grabbed the cuff with her free hand and tucked her thumb into her palm and pulled her other hand against the metal, trying to wiggle it free. She stared at the door, willing him not to come back. After a few moments, with no sign of his returning footsteps, she finally pulled her hand free.

She stood up and peered out the window. She could see Steele walking in the moonlight outside, heading toward the beach. If she could sneak downstairs and get out the front door, which was on the opposite side of the cabin, maybe she could get away.

She pulled on the clothes Raven had brought her earlier, then walked to the door. She pulled it open and peered into the hall. The way was clear, so she slipped from the room and tiptoed down the stairs.

As she stepped toward the door and reached for the doorknob, she saw a shadow in the window. Oh, God, Steele must be returning. She leaped back from the door and scurried into the kitchen. She raced into the room, then peered out the door to the hallway, waiting to see if the front door would open.

If Steele came in, she only had minutes before he realized she'd escaped. As soon as he went up the stairs, she'd hurry and slip out the front door, then disappear into the woods.

"Fuck, it's good to see you, baby."

At the sound of Steele's voice behind her, she gasped, and would have spun around, but his strong arms came around her waist and he pulled her tight to his body. His cock pressed into her back as his lips nuzzled her neck.

She could barely catch her breath. He turned her around and in the shadowy kitchen, claimed her lips. His tongue dove into her mouth, opening her lips wide as he explored her mouth. His tongue swirled inside her, forcing her jaw wider. She could taste the liquor on him.

His hands stroked down her back, then cupped her ass and he pulled her tight to his body, his erection grinding against her sex.

"Baby, I need a good fuck, and I need it now."

She panicked as she heard the sound of a zipper.

She started to protest, but his lips covered hers again, his tongue demanding. She struggled against the big body pinning her to the wooden door.

"Oh, yeah, baby. Fight me. I like that." He grabbed a

handful of her T-shirt and pulled it from her jeans, then slid his hand underneath and cupped her breast.

His tongue slid into her mouth again, preventing her protest. His hand moved down her side, then he unzipped her jeans. When his big hand slid down her belly, then dipped into her panties, she panicked and struggled harder.

She whimpered against his mouth. In one second, he would know she was wet. She hated it, but being in his arms upstairs, and now his dominant control of her . . . Was it a sickness that being dominated by a strong man turned her on? Her experience with Donovan should have cured her of that completely.

His finger brushed against her slick folds and she wanted to moan in pleasure.

"Fuck, you're so wet."

His hand slipped from her slickness and then she felt hot, hard flesh brush against her.

She shook her head until she freed her mouth.

She sucked in a breath. "No, don't do this. Please."

"Ah, fuck, Raven. You sure?"

"I'm . . . not . . . Raven," she said between gasps.

His big body, which still pinned her to the door, stiffened. She could feel her own body trembling.

He drew his head back and stared down at her. She could barely see his face in the shadowy room, but in the hint of moonlight she could tell he was frowning.

"Fuck. What the hell are you doing out of the room?" He grasped her shoulders and squeezed. "How did you get out of the cuffs?"

She just glared at him.

His eyes narrowed as he drew back. "So what was your plan? Sneak out in the middle of the night? Try to walk back to town?" He shook her again. "I already told you there are bears out there. And God knows what other kind of predators."

"You mean like you?"

"I thought you were Raven." He scowled and grabbed her by the shoulders, then turned her roughly. "Hell, I don't need to explain to you."

She zipped up her jeans as he prodded her forward, then he dragged her down the hall and up the stairs. He said nothing until he shoved her into the bedroom and closed the door behind him. He flicked on the switch by the door and the lamp came on.

"I should just let you go, right now. Let you figure out whatever mess you find yourself in. There's no reason me or my men should wind up in trouble because of you." He grabbed her shoulders and glared at her. "But you'd prob- ably turn us in to the police, and charge us with kidnap- ping, even though we were only trying to help." He stared at her. "I really want to just kick your pretty little ass out of here, but I can't do that."

He grabbed the key from the dresser and unfastened the cuff from the headboard, then he grabbed her arm and pulled her toward him, then snapped the cuff around her wrist.

"Take off your jeans."

Obediently, she dropped them to the floor, shivering, but not daring to argue with him.

He walked behind her and pushed up the back of her T-shirt. She gasped. He unfastened the hooks of her bra, then walked in front of her again. She stared at him nervously.

"You don't want to sleep in that thing, do you? Take it off."

She didn't want to pull off the T-shirt, then remove the bra because it was clear he wasn't going to look away, so she wrestled her way out of the first strap by pulling it out the sleeve, then pulling her arm into the sleeve enough to pull the strap over her hand. She freed the second strap, though it was a little harder with the handcuffs dangling from her wrist, then she reached under the shirt and pulled out the bra. Her nipples pushed against the fabric and his gaze flickered to them.

"Lie down," he commanded.

She sat down on the bed, watching him warily. He clamped his big hand around her uncuffed arm and pulled it over her head, then he grabbed the empty cuff attached to her other wrist and pulled it around a post on the headboard. The cold steel clamped around her second wrist.

He walked to the dresser and shoved the key in the top drawer.

"I tried to be nice before. Immobilize just one of your arms. But if I can't trust you not to run off in the middle of the night, I'll have to be more cautious. And less generous."

He dropped his jeans to the floor and stepped out of

them, then shed his shirt. His big cock was still swollen, barely contained in his snug boxers.

"Fuck, do you know how hard it is sleeping beside you and not doing anything about it? And you look so fucking sexy lying like that."

With her arms pulled over her head, her breasts were thrust upward, and with his intense gaze on them, her nipples peaked, pushing against the fabric.

He sank onto the chair facing the bed and pulled his cock free, then wrapped his hand around the considerable length. He began to stroke, watching her, his eyes intense. She couldn't help staring at the massive shaft as his hand glided up and down, stimulating it. God, if she weren't his prisoner, she would love to get up and kneel down in front of him, then wrap her hand around it and stroke, just like he was doing now. She'd love to capture that huge cockhead in her mouth and suck. Feel the hard flesh fill her mouth.

Damn, what was wrong with her? Her insides quivered. Oh, God, if he unfastened her cuffs right now and commanded her to sink to her knees in front of him and suck him to climax, then swallow every drop, she would do it. She *wanted* to do it.

And that's why she hated herself right now.

She watched transfixed as he picked up his rhythm, pumping himself harder and faster. The only sound in the room was his heavy breathing and the sound of skin moving roughly over skin. She felt her own breathing accelerate in time with his bobbing fist. Then he groaned and, as she watched, a stream of white erupted from his cock, then spilled down over his hand, which still jerked up and down. Her insides tightened at the thought of what it would feel like if his cock had been deep inside her when he'd come.

He grabbed a tissue and wiped himself up, then disappeared into the bathroom. When he returned a few moments later, he turned out the light, then climbed into bed behind her.

"Fuck, roll over."

She started to roll toward him.

"No, the other way. I'm not going to be tortured all night by the sight of those pert breasts of yours pointing at the ceiling."

He moved close and his arm came around her waist, then he drew her tight to his body.

"With your hands cuffed like that, you're bound to roll onto your back again when you fall asleep. I don't want that to happen."

His arm tightened around her waist and with her arms pulled over her head, she wouldn't be able to stop him from brushing his hands over her breasts if he wanted to. His big fingers were only inches from them.

And, God help her, she really wanted him to reach up and cup her breasts in his big hands.

Her heart thundered and she waited, but then his deep, even breathing told her he'd fallen asleep.

This man had been responsible for kidnapping her. He kept her trapped in this cabin, and handcuffed to his bed.

But he could have taken her anytime he wanted—and he'd definitely wanted to—but he hadn't.

He seemed to be an honorable man. And she almost believed she could trust him.

And that thinking was exactly why she knew that tomorrow she had to find a way to escape.

The first thing Laurie sensed was that there was no longer a hard, muscular body behind her. Then she had the feeling someone was watching her. She opened her eyes and found herself staring at the ceiling. Her shoulders ached and when she shifted, she felt the pinch of metal around her wrists.

"I'm sorry about last night," Steele said.

Her gaze darted to Steele, sitting on the same chair where he'd found his release last night, but this time he was fully clothed, and looked quite intimidating with his bulging shoulder muscles brimming from the very short sleeves of his T-shirt, his snake tattoo coiling down his arm.

He stood up and walked toward the bed, then released her wrists. She lowered her arms slowly against the aching muscles, then rubbed her wrists, ever conscious of his hard, masculine body so close.

"I had too much to drink and downstairs I thought you were Raven, or I never would have . . ."

She nodded. "I know. I get it. And you were mad that I tried to escape."

He sighed and stepped away from the bed. "I wish you'd believe me that we're trying to help you."

Now that his big, intimidating body had moved away from the bed, she sat up, frowning.

"Most people don't go this far out of their way to help someone else."

His gaze caught hers. "I'm not most people." Then he turned away and walked toward the door.

"Get dressed and come down. Breakfast is almost ready."

When Laurie went down to sit at the table, she found that everyone was present. At least, everyone she knew about, including Dom and Magic. Afterward, she helped to clear away the dishes and offered to help clean up. Shock assigned her to do the dishes.

Over the meal, the others had talked about going out for a ride. As she placed a plate in the dish drainer, Steele came into the kitchen.

"We're all going out except Dom and Magic. They're staying here to watch you."

She nodded and placed another clean plate in the drainer. She watched from the kitchen window as the men mounted their bikes. Raven climbed on behind Rip and the bikes roared to life, then they drove off down the long gravel driveway and disappeared beyond the trees. Magic and Dom sat on the deck outside.

Since Steele hadn't chained her to the kitchen sink, it seemed he trusted she wouldn't just run off. Of course, with Magic and Dom sitting right there, it wasn't as if she could slip away without them seeing her. And what would she do if she did get away?

Ten minutes later, she finished the dishes and dried her hands, then glanced out the window again. Dom and Magic were gone. She headed back to the living room and peered into the room.

She saw Dom dealing some cards while Magic took a swig from a beer bottle, a thorny tattoo around his right wrist. Words in script, like an incantation of some kind, spiraled up his arm. His dark brown hair, cropped short on the sides and longer on the top, was tousled today, rather than combed back like he'd worn it yesterday.

Dom picked up his cards. Sunlight glinted from a steel skull ring on his finger. He glanced at his cards and stroked his hand over his scalp, which was covered with short bristly hair. A one-inch scar slashed across his chin, partially covered by the fringe of hair that formed a line along the edge of his chin from temple to temple.

Laurie kept out of view, wondering how long they would play cards before they grew concerned about her whereabouts.

This was her golden opportunity. They were busy and totally heedless of her, assuming she was working on that pile of dishes in the kitchen. She was sure it wouldn't be too long before they came to check on her, so she had to make her move now.

She tiptoed silently along the hall toward the kitchen, then quietly opened the back door and slipped outside.

She dodged to the left and peered around the house. All but two of the bikes were gone and she didn't see anyone around. Dom and Magic had a view of the beach, but they wouldn't see her out here. Still, she moved quickly and headed for cover, straight to the path that led to where Raven had gone swimming yesterday. She raced past the clearing where she had watched Raven with the other men, remembering Steele's big body pressed to her back, then watching him fucking Raven in the water, right alongside the other two men.

She sucked in air and kept on moving, well aware that there were other paths leading to this place. Dom and Magic had approached the small beach from a different direction than she had. Rather than following one of the worn side paths she saw, once she put a little more distance between her and the cabin, she turned into the woods and headed for the water's edge, then followed it as best she could.

They'd be less likely to find her here, and if she heard them coming, there were many places for her to duck and hide. And the water should eventually lead her to a road, or another cabin, or something. But her biggest concern right now was to get away from the men who held her captive. Walking along a road would make it far too easy for them to spot her.

She could wait to find a safe haven.

But the going was hard, and several hours later, when she was exhausted from hiking through brush, and hungry, she started to worry.

Then it started to rain. And not just a little. It came down in buckets, soaking her to the skin. The grass was slippery to walk on. She wiped water from her eyes, her aching muscles protesting as she plodded along.

She spotted a clearing ahead. She turned toward it, stepping faster, and found a small parking area, devoid of cars. She'd seen a few of these along the way, but had avoided them. This time, she followed the gravel path leading to the parking area, knowing it would take her to the road.

She approached the road and heard a car go by, and then another. Oh, God, would the bikers be out looking for her in this heavy rain? She stepped toward the trees lining the roadside and peered through them.

Her heart leaped as she saw the most beautiful sight she'd ever seen.

A police car!

It had been stopped on the side of the road several yards ahead, but now it started to pull away. *Oh, God, no.*

She raced to the roadside and began to wave her arms, but the rain was so heavy, and maybe the driver just wasn't checking his rearview mirror, because he started driving forward.

She dashed onto the narrow road and ran after him, but water was flooding from the paved surface with the onslaught of rain from the heavens, and her foot slipped on the slick surface, sending her tumbling to the ground. At the same time, the car did a U-turn, and headed in her direction.

Oh, God, if the driver didn't see her . . . She tried to scramble to her feet as the headlights approached, then sucked in a breath. But the car stopped.

A tall officer in a slick raincoat stepped toward her.

"Are you all right, ma'am?" he asked, staring down at her with concern in his dark eyes.

"No, officer. I'm not." Tears welled in her eyes.

Collide

"It's all right, ma'am," the officer said to Laurie as he held out his hand to her.

She took it and he helped her to her feet, then with a steady arm on her elbow, guided her to the squad car. He opened the back door and she slipped inside. He closed the door and walked toward the back of the car. She could hear the trunk open, then a moment later he got into the driver's seat. He turned and handed her a blanket.

She took it with trembling hands and wrapped it around herself. Her clothes were soaked right through.

The policeman settled into the driver's seat. "What's your name, ma'am?"

"My name is Laurie Conners." She leaned forward and glanced at the reflection of his face in the rearview mirror, but he was looking down at his cell phone, texting something. "And I've got to tell you, there are these men . . . bikers . . . and they're looking for me. In fact—"

"Do you believe you're in danger?" he asked.

"I . . . uh . . . well, they kidnapped me."

He put away his phone and glanced at her in the mirror. "That's a serious accusation. Do you want to press charges?"

She had told Steele she wouldn't charge him, but she'd said it to convince him to let her go. But, did she want to press charges?

She shook her head. "No. I just want to go . . ." She was going to say home, but she realized that Steele and Wild Card were right. Donovan would probably be looking for her there. "I want to go somewhere safe."

He put the car in gear and started moving. The windshield wipers slapped back and forth, clearing the sheet of water that steadily poured across the glass, but they could barely see past the front of the car.

Laurie huddled into the blanket and sank back in the seat, feeling safe for the first time in a long time. Not just since Steele and his men had kidnapped her, but in the several months she'd been dating Donovan.

She pulled the blanket closer. How had she let things go so far with Donovan?

She'd wanted to trust Donovan. He was rich, successful. Handsome. He was the perfect man. At least on the surface. But when she'd started having second thoughts, her girlfriends told her she was just afraid of commitment. When she first realized he had some kinky tastes in the bedroom, it had unnerved her a little, but every article she read about sex said that couples should let loose and try new and different things. He was more experienced than her and so was ahead of her in that department. At least, that's what she'd tried to convince herself. At first, it had been a bit of bondage, then he'd started giving her orders. She had been shocked at how mindlessly and completely she had responded to his domination. A part of her craved being controlled and that scared her a little. But she'd been willing to push back her other issues to explore this side of herself.

Then things had taken a strange turn.

She had been staying with him for the weekend at a big house he had in the country. The house was beautiful, but she didn't get to enjoy it much. The first day, he'd dragged her into a small bedroom and bound her wrists and ankles to the bed, then had sex with her. Then he'd just left her there.

A couple of hours later, he'd come back and taken her again, then given her some food. When it became clear he wasn't going to let her free, she told him she wanted to end this, but he simply said, "Silence, slave," and shoved a ball gag into her mouth. He'd fucked her one more time that evening, then left her alone in the darkness all night long.

In the morning, he'd dragged her from the bed and bound her to what he called a punishment bench, where she was bent over the padded, wooden frame, forcing her naked ass into the air, then he'd slapped her. Hard. Over and over again until her ass burned.

Afterward, when she'd told him how upset his actions had made her, he'd apologized, telling her he'd thought she'd wanted the whole immersion scenario, that he'd thought it had turned her on. He'd promised that he'd be more careful in the future.

She'd reluctantly continued seeing him, but he was attentive and seemed genuinely sorry for his mistake in judgment. For a while. But then they had slipped back into the Dominant-submissive roles and things started to derail again. What caused her to finally break it off with him was when during sex, he'd wrapped his hands around her neck and squeezed so tight, she'd almost passed out. He'd seemed to enjoy the total panic in her eyes, and her obvious sense of complete helplessness. That was the final straw.

She sank into the seat and let the movement of the car lull her as she watched the water stream down the window beside her. She was safe now. She shivered inside. At least, from the bikers.

She seemed to have dozed off because she awoke with a start when the car came to a stop. She peered out the window but the rain hadn't let up and everything outside was blurred. But it didn't look like she was at a police station. She thought she could make out trees, and some shadowy shapes approached the car.

The officer in the front seat glanced back at her in the mirror.

"Wait here, ma'am." He opened the car door and stepped out.

"Hey, Killer. So you found her?"

She stiffened. That sounded like Rip's voice.

A moment later, the door beside her swung open and Steele glared at her.

"What the hell were you thinking?"

The policeman put his arm in front of Steele. "Now, Steele, give her a minute until you cool off."

Steele's eyes narrowed. "Screw that." He grabbed her wrist and tugged her from the car. Her heart pounded loudly as he dragged her into the house.

"Why did that police officer bring me back here when I told him you kidnapped me?" she asked as he tugged her up the stairs. "And how did he know you were here?"

"Killer is a friend of your brother's."

They reached the top of the stairs and he pulled her down the hall.

"Killer? Is he even a real cop?" she asked.

"People around here know him as Officer Grainger, but Rip knew him when he was an undercover cop in a criminal gang. Killer was his ride name. About six months ago, he decided he'd had enough of that life. He moved here with his new wife and became friends with your brother."

He pushed her into the bedroom and slammed the door behind him. "But that's not what I want to talk about right now."

He stared at her, his breathing heavy. They both stood there dripping on the hardwood floor.

"I'm going to ask you again, what the hell were you thinking?" he demanded.

The expression on his face was more anxious than angry, she realized, but when he took a step toward her, she jerked back.

"Ah, fuck, really?" He glared at her as he strode closer. "I've done everything I can to prove to you that I won't take you against your will, but you still don't believe me." He stepped closer and she backed up until the wall pressed against her.

He stood so close that if she took a deep breath her breasts would brush his big, solid chest.

His eyes narrowed. "Since you've already tried and convicted me in your mind maybe I should just commit the crime."

He cupped her face with one big hand and tipped up her chin, then captured her lips. A moment later, he whispered against her mouth. "But I would never do that. Do you understand me, Laurie?" Then his tongue drove into her mouth with a sure stroke, claiming her for his own. Tears streamed from her eyes because she wanted to relax into his arms and invite him to take her. She wanted him to hold her close, to feel the comfort of his body. She could feel his cock hard against her belly and she wanted to open to him and feel him glide inside.

He seemed like such a good man. He seemed to care about her.

But then so had Donovan. At first.

Steele's mouth moved on hers, his body shifting closer, pinning her to the wall.

Their lips parted and he stared at her, his glittering granite eyes boring through her.

"Fuck, I was worried something had happened to you. That you were lost, maybe hurt."

The concern in his eyes tore at her gut. Did he really care?

"I was lost. I was so glad . . ." Her throat closed up and tears welled. ". . . to . . . to see that police car on the road and flag it down. If he hadn't stopped . . ." She sobbed. She had just felt so alone and terrified out in the woods alone, not knowing how to find her way back.

His strong arms tightened around her and she leaned against him, taking comfort in his closeness. Her heart thumped loudly against him and she could hear the echo of his. He drew back and cupped both her cheeks, then lowered his face to hers. The brush of his lips was soft and gentle and they moved on hers with a tenderness that shocked her, sliding past all her barriers, and she found herself responding. His tongue slid into her mouth and she stroked it with hers. He held her tight to his muscular body and her nipples, already hard from the cold and wet, felt an agony of need as they bored into his rock-solid chest.

He drew back and stared at her, looking as bewildered as she was.

He sucked in a breath and stepped back. "You need to get out of those wet clothes."

She stared up at him, ready to surrender to her need at last. To strip off her clothes at his command and let him take her, whatever the consequences.

She reached for the hem of her T-shirt and pulled it

over her head, exposing her wet, lace-clad breasts to his view.

"What the hell are you doing? You fucking overestimate my self-control." He grasped her shoulders and turned her around, then marched her to the bathroom door. "Get in there, strip down, and have a hot bath. I'll be back in a few minutes with something to warm you up."

She couldn't help hoping the *something* was him. After all her fighting against the idea, now that she'd given up the fight, she couldn't wait to be in his arms again. To feel his powerful body against hers. To finally feel his big cock glide into her.

When she finished her bath and returned to the bedroom wrapped in a big, fluffy towel, he was sitting in the armchair.

"I brought you a hot chocolate." He stood and picked up a metal thermal mug from the dresser and handed it to her. She took a sip. It was still piping hot.

"When you're finished with that, get dressed and come downstairs. Officer Grainger wants to talk to you."

Laurie walked down the stairs and into the living room to see Officer Grainger sitting at the dining room table sipping a cup of coffee. Sitting with him was Rip, Wild Card, and Steele. Shock, Raven, Magic, and Dom were relaxing in the living room.

She crossed the room and sat in the empty chair across from the police officer.

"Miss Connors . . . Laurie . . . May I call you Laurie?"

She nodded numbly.

"I think you and I should have a talk. I think you should fully understand the situation you're in."

Wild Card picked up the thermos of coffee on the table and filled a mug for her. She sipped it, letting the heat emanate through her.

"Laurie, I'm sure you must be confused by all of this. I just want you to know that these men are your friends and they are looking out for you. We believe that if you were to go back home now, you'd be in danger."

She nodded, frowning. "I know Donovan is a problem, and I really don't want to see him again, but I can't stay here forever."

After the way he'd behaved, and from their history, she was apprehensive of what Donovan might do, but she had to find a way to move forward.

"I really think it's in your best interest to wait until your brother gets back."

"Steele told me you and Craig are friends," she said.

Whereas Laurie chose to live in Jasmineville, a small city, Craig lived in a small town called Marin Falls, about an hour out, preferring the quieter lifestyle. He owned a sporting goods store in the town and Laurie drove out a couple of times a month for Sunday dinner, but she didn't know Craig's friends.

"That's right, and I've been trying to get in touch with him to let him know what's happened, but without success."

He folded his hands on the table.

"A while ago, Craig told me you're in a relationship with Donovan Blake and he also told me he's had concerns about this man for quite a while."

"He's always been overly protective of me," she said.

"Well, this time it seems justified," Officer Grainger said. "I ran a search on Donovan, and I was shocked at what I found."

She wrapped her hands around the coffee mug, finding comfort in its warmth, not wanting to hear what he was about to say.

"This is not the kind of man you want to tangle with. He's been charged with assaulting several women, but he always managed to get the charges dropped. Every one of the women had been in a relationship with him, and had said things just kept getting worse. By the time the assault happened, they had all wanted out of the relationship, but were intimidated by him, and were afraid of what he'd do to them if they walked away."

She knew she was trembling. His intense gaze locked on hers.

"Then one woman almost died of asphyxiation."

The breath froze in her lungs. She could remember Donovan's hands around her throat. Remembered the terrifying feeling of being unable to breathe. Thank God he'd found his release before she'd passed out, or worse.

"She was terrified and her family talked her into pressing charges against him. But this man is well connected and has money. He finally convinced her to drop the charges, probably with a big payoff. Just after that, he moved to this area.

"Over the course of four years, two women he dated disappeared. No one could ever prove a connection between their disappearances and him, but the circumstances are highly suspicious."

"Are you saying you think he . . . murdered them?"

"I'm not making any allegations, but I do think he's dangerous."

Her gaze fell on Wild Card, whose jaw tightened in obvious anger, and then to Rip, who watched her with an assessing eye. Probably trying to gauge her reaction to Officer Grainger's revelations.

"There's more. I want you to understand that the women he hurt weren't just beaten once by him. They were abused on an ongoing basis, every one of them afraid to leave him for fear of what he might do to them. That's why Craig wanted to get you away from him. He was going to tell you about what I discovered when he got back, but he had a bad feeling about the other night when you were going out to celebrate an anniversary. That's why Steele and his crew went to the bar that night. To make sure you were okay."

None of what Officer Grainger told her about Donovan came as a huge surprise to her. Not really. Not after having experienced Donovan's mistreatment. But she hated sitting there like a child, being made to understand how dire her predicament was.

She felt helpless and resentful. Of Donovan, of course,

but also of these men who sat here judging her stupidity at having gotten herself involved with such a man. Not that any of them said it. But she knew they were thinking it. Just like Craig had thought it.

It only made it worse that he was right.

Officer Grainger leaned forward. "Laurie, I know he's probably been more careful since he's been here. That last incident was enough to send him packing. To go somewhere that people didn't know him. But he'll fall into old habits."

She straightened in her chair. "So what you're saying is, I really have no choice. Stay here or go back home and fear retaliation from the man I was in a relationship with."

The bitter resentment in her voice was clear. She felt trapped. And controlled by these men who claimed to want to protect her.

She knew deep inside that none of this was their fault, and that they were just trying to help, but that didn't change how she felt.

Silence hung in the air.

She felt cold. And numb. Her throat was tight and she couldn't talk. Not that she had anything she wanted to say.

Right now, she just wanted to escape. Not out the door to return home. That was the last thing she wanted right now.

She wanted to escape her life. Escape her stupidity at ever having gone out with Donovan, let alone staying with him.

And she wanted to escape from these men's judging gazes.

She tightened her arms, which were folded around her, and pushed herself to her feet.

Steele's gaze stayed locked on her. Assessing her. Judging her.

"Where are you going?" he asked.

She drew in a shaky breath and forced herself to speak. "Upstairs."

She could feel tears prickling at her eyes. She didn't want these men to see her being so weak.

"Are you okay, Laurie?" Shock asked.

She nodded her head, barely trusting her voice not to break.

She walked away from the table to the entrance, her pace increasing as she neared the stairway, then she hurried up the stairs, stopping herself from fleeing in an all-out run.

She reached the bedroom and opened the door, then closed it behind her. She leaned against it, barely able to hold back the tears. She caught her breath, then pushed herself away and walked to the bed, feeling numb inside. She lay down, pulled her knees tight to her chest, and clung to them.

Her body ached from walking so much today, especially through the rough terrain. And when she thought of the mess she was in, her stomach quivered and her mind whirled.

And her heart ached.

Why couldn't she attract a nice man? So far, she'd only attracted men who didn't really care about her, or in Donovan's case, actively wanted to hurt her.

Even kill her.

She'd been alone in an isolated house with Donovan when he'd choked her. She'd been chained and couldn't fight him. If he'd gone too far, like he had with that other woman . . .

He could have killed her. Then he would have just gotten rid of her body and paid off anyone who questioned his word that he hadn't seen her that weekend.

Someone tapped at the door.

"Laurie, may I come in?" Steele said from the other side of the door.

She couldn't believe he was asking permission.

But she didn't say anything. Her throat was too choked up. And what could she say? No? He wouldn't accept that.

The door opened and he peered inside. When he saw her curled up on the bed, he pushed the door open and entered.

"I just wanted to make sure you're all right." He closed the door behind him. "I know Killer gave you a lot to think about."

She began to tremble from head to toe. She was in this impossible situation. She couldn't go home, because Donovan might hurt her, and her only option was to stay here with these men who had kidnapped her.

He stepped farther into the room. "Do you want to talk about it?"

"And say what?" She was surprised at how even her voice sounded. "Admit that I'm an idiot for having gotten involved with the man? To cry about the fact that now I'm in trouble and that my brother was right all along and if only I'd listened to him . . ." She ran out of air and sucked in a deep breath.

Steele walked toward the bed. "Laurie, it's not your fault. Guys like that . . . they have a way to pull people in. You're the victim here. You've done nothing to deserve this, understand?"

Tears welled from her eyes and she curled tighter.

He sat down on the bed behind her, resting his hand on her shoulder. The warmth of his touch was comforting. A sob escaped her throat.

"He was so charming at first." She sucked in a breath. "He made me feel like the most important person in the world. I hadn't been with anyone in a while . . . I'd had a bad breakup with a guy who didn't really care about being with me . . . I was just convenient. So when Donovan treated me like I was someone special . . ." She choked up again, but took in a deep breath and relaxed her throat. "And he took charge. I liked that." She hugged her knees tighter. "At first."

Steele didn't say anything, just squeezed her shoulder reassuringly.

"Craig never liked him. He hadn't even met him, but he started on about how I shouldn't be with him. It was as if he didn't trust a guy who thought I was special."

She shook her head. "And he was right. I was so stupid."

"You're not stupid to think someone would find you special." He squeezed her shoulder again, and warmth emanated through her. "And I'm sure that's not what your brother meant. He cares about you."

She just nodded, barely hearing him, tumultuous emotions swirling through her. "When things started going wrong . . . they were just little at first, you know? . . . but Craig kept pushing me to drop the guy, but my friends kept telling me he was great and I was lucky to be dating a rich, handsome guy who seemed to adore me."

"What kind of things started going wrong?" he asked.

She sniffed and shook her head. She didn't want to tell hm. Didn't want to admit just how stupid she'd been.

But she needed to tell someone. She let out a pent-up breath.

"He liked to dominate me. In the bedroom." She closed her eyes and bowed her head. "I know it sounds stupid that I let him."

"Did you enjoy it?"

She stiffened.

He sighed, and his hand stroked back some hair that had fallen across her cheek. "I didn't mean that as a criticism. There's nothing wrong with enjoying giving up control to someone. Or taking it. As long as that's what you both want."

"I did. I mean, I found it . . ." Her stomach quivered, but she wanted to tell the truth. To tell someone. "Exciting. It was strange, but he was so in control and confident.

I found that . . . sexy." She sucked in a breath. "But it was also a little scary."

"Why?"

"He . . . liked to bind me. Sometimes with rope. Sometimes with leather restraints or handcuffs. But I had no way to tell him when I didn't want him to do something. He liked me to pretend to struggle against him, so saying no became part of the playacting."

"You didn't have a safe word?"

"I . . ." She shook her head. "I didn't know about . . . I mean, I'd never done anything like that before."

"*You* shouldn't have had to know. He should have." He stroked her back. "And I'm sure he did. He was getting off on controlling you, but not in a healthy Dom-sub relationship. He was enjoying your fear."

Tears welled in her eyes again and she squeezed her legs tighter to her chest, resting her face on her knees.

"Aw, sweetheart, it's not your fault." He pushed himself onto the bed beside her and scooped her up, pulling her onto his lap. His big arms came around her and she found her head resting against his solid, welcoming chest. He rocked her as she sobbed in his arms, her head tucked under his chin. He was so strong, and she felt protected in his embrace.

"My friends told me I just wasn't used to kinky play in the bedroom and I was overreacting. Of course, I didn't tell them all of it."

"Like what, Laurie? Tell me."

She gazed up at him, worried at how he would perceive her. She didn't want him to think she was stupid or weak, when he was so strong. She admired Steele.

"He would punish me. Which I know is something that turns some people on. I thought maybe I was just being too stuffy. At first, he'd spank me with his hand. I didn't like it, but it turned him on, so I decided to push my limits and go with it. Then he started using a flogger of some kind. One day, I told him I didn't like it . . . before we got started, you know? He seemed annoyed, but he agreed not to use it. Instead, he brought out a riding crop and struck me again and again, so hard it burned. I had trouble sitting for days after."

Steele must have been wondering why she hadn't stopped seeing Donovan then. Why she'd been such an idiot. But he just stroked her back. And held her close.

"What made you finally decide to break it off with him?" Steele asked.

She began to tremble in his arms. "It was . . . He had me handcuffed to a . . . what he called a punishment bench. When he was . . ." She drew in a breath, remembering Donovan behind her, driving deep into her body in hard strokes. "Like . . . in the middle of things. He wrapped his hands around my neck."

Her fingers curled tight, grasping the fabric of Steele's shirt.

"I couldn't breathe. And he just kept . . ." She couldn't say it out loud. "I felt panicky. I thought, if he didn't . . . uh . . . find . . . his release . . . I was afraid I'd pass out. That maybe I wouldn't wake up again."

Steele's arms tightened around her.

"Sweetheart, you're safe now."

But she wasn't. Donovan was still out there, and eventually she had to leave here and face him. And she didn't know what he'd do to her.

"You're safe here," he said again, murmuring against her hair.

And she did feel safe in his arms. She wished she never had to leave them. She shifted on his lap and wrapped her arms around him, holding him close. Never wanting to let him go.

Steele's heart ached as Laurie burrowed deep into his arms. She was so fragile right now. So vulnerable.

That jackass had really done a number on her, and if he ever got his hands on the guy, he would likely kill him. At the fierceness of his thought, he held her tight, and she whimpered a little. He eased his hold on her and kissed the crown of her head.

"It's all right. I'll never hurt you. You know that, don't you?"

She nodded, filling him with a deep sense of satisfaction.

But he would have to make sure he never got his hands on that Donovan asshole. The last thing he needed was another assault-and-battery charge on his record.

Or possibly manslaughter.

Steele heard her murmuring in the bed. Once she'd fallen asleep, he'd moved to the armchair, giving her space. In the darkness, though, her whimpers made him want to go to her, and he was just about to throw the blanket he'd pulled over himself aside when she sat bolt upright, with a strangled "No."

She sucked in rapid breaths of air and glanced around. His eyes were used to the darkness, but she probably couldn't see him in the shadowy depths.

"Are you all right, Laurie?"

"Steele?" Her head turned in his direction.

She pushed back the covers and, for a confused moment, he thought she was going to bolt, but instead of heading for the door, she hurried toward him and—to his total surprise—climbed onto his lap and flung her arms around him, then snuggled against his body.

She was like a tiny child who'd woken up frightened in the night and needed comfort. He wrapped his arms around her and held her close. Her head rested against his shoulder and her soft breath brushed against his cheek. She was trembling—because she was cold or frightened because of the dream she'd been having, he wasn't sure, but probably the latter. He tugged the blanket from his knees and wrapped it around her. Within moments, she was asleep again, so he just held her.

Light washed against Laurie's eyes and she opened them. She was in Steele's big solid arms, on his lap in an armchair.

Reminding her how she'd trotted to him in the middle of the night like a child seeking comfort. But she didn't feel like a child now, snuggled against his muscular body, his strong arms encircling her.

He glanced down at her. "Good morning."

"Morning."

He was so close. So masculine. Their faces were only inches apart. She gazed into his intense gray eyes, drawn in deeper and deeper. The two of them seemed to be drawn together by some magnetic force and his lips found hers. His mouth moved on hers tenderly, totally undemanding. Need welled up in her and she wrapped her arms around his neck and drew him closer.

When they finally parted, their gazes were locked. She wanted him to carry her to the bed and make love to her. To make her feel what it was like to be with someone who cared about her.

She drew back with a start. How did she know this man cared about her?

"Is there something wrong?"

She shook her head.

He obviously had a basic respect for her and her needs, but it wasn't a caring for her like a man for a woman in a relationship. She didn't even know him. She was projecting her need to be protected and cared for onto this man who was basically her captor.

He was a good man. She knew that now. But he didn't love her. He simply felt a responsibility to keep her safe.

And she also believed he felt as intense an attraction for her as she felt for him.

She stroked her hand across the defined muscles of his chest, wishing there could be more between them. Still, it didn't mean she couldn't appreciate all he'd done for her.

"Steele, thank you for looking out for me, and for keeping me safe despite my best efforts to break away."

"Escape, you mean?" He grinned. "Truth be told, that's one of the things I love about you. Your tenacity."

Love?

He didn't mean that the way her pounding heart wanted him to. *Did he?*

Shock zipped through her. Could she really want him to fall in love with her? This man she'd only met days ago? After he'd kidnapped her?

But the kidnapping made him all the more appealing because it showed the lengths to which he'd go to keep her safe.

"What are you thinking?" he asked, watching her changing expressions.

"I just realized that everything about our relationship has changed."

His eyebrow arched. "Relationship?"

"Well, you know . . . I mean . . ." But she noticed his eyes were glittering with amusement.

"Yes, I know. I'm no longer the big bad man who has you chained to his bed." He grinned and kissed her lips lightly.

She smiled timidly at him. "True. But you know, if I had to find myself trapped in someone's bed, I'm glad it was yours."

Fire blazed in his eyes and he drew her close, his lips ravaging hers.

"Steele," someone said while rapping on the door.

Steele tore his lips from hers. "Fuck," he muttered under his breath, then snarled, "What do you want?"

"Laurie's brother is on the phone. He wants to talk to her."

He stared at her. "This isn't over."

She smiled and slipped from his lap.

Sometime during the night, she'd shed her jeans, so she quickly pulled them on as Steele walked to the door. He opened it, revealing Rip standing in the doorway.

Rip handed him a cell phone and Steele nodded, then closed the door and handed the phone to Laurie.

"Hello?" she said.

"Laurie, I'm glad you're okay. I heard about what happened," Craig said on the other end of the line.

She didn't know which happening he referred to, and she didn't care right now.

"You've been out of town," she said.

"Yeah, I had to go on business, but I got back as soon as I could."

"But you were busy before you left." Her hand tightened on the phone.

"What do you mean?"

"I mean, arranging for my kidnapping."

"Laurie, wait—"

"No, I'm not going to wait. How could you do that?" She was aware of Steele in the background, watching her.

"I was just trying to keep you safe. And you must know that I made that suggestion when I was . . . uh . . . less than sober."

"But sober or not, you really thought that turning me over to a gang of bikers was a reasonable solution?"

"I didn't turn you over to a gang of bikers. I asked my friend—a cop—to help me look out for you. He knew these guys and one of them is an ex-cop, too. I knew you'd be in good hands. Anyway, I told you, I was drunk at the time, and desperate to protect you. But none of that matters, because they refused."

"And yet, here I am," she responded, her hand balling into a fist. But she realized that it wasn't fair to pin that on her brother, since it was circumstances that had caused Wild Card to snatch her. And save her from Donovan's clutches, she admitted to herself. Her gaze darted to Steele.

But despite that, she couldn't let her brother get away with this kind of thing.

"Craig, you really can't do things like this. You're overprotective and controlling. I need to live my own life. I'm an intelligent adult."

"Are you sure?" he asked, annoyance in his voice. "Because some of your choices suggest otherwise."

Anger flared inside her and she jabbed the END button, then spiked the phone at the armchair. It hit the cushion then bounced to the floor as she tugged the bedroom door open and stormed out. She strode down the stairs then straight out the front door. She ignored the stares of Dom, Rip, and Shock who sat in chairs on the grass overlooking the water and continued along the path to the isolated beach. She kept walking until the glittering water came into view and past the dense bushes then stopped by a big tree and leaned back against it, waiting for her pounding heart to settle down.

"You okay?" Steele asked from behind her.

"Afraid I'd run away?" she asked, annoyance in her voice.

But he ignored her barb. "I thought you might want to talk." He stepped closer. "Your brother cares about you. You know that."

She drew in a deep breath. "Yet he arranged for you to kidnap me."

"He wasn't really serious, and we didn't go along with it."

She glared at him. "And yet I'm here."

He walked toward her. "Laurie, don't transfer your anger at your brother to me. You know what happened." He grasped her shoulders and gazed at her, his granite eyes intense. "Wild Card—or any of us, for that matter—wouldn't have ignored what was happening to you in that parking garage. He stepped in because he wouldn't just stand by and allow that asshole to manhandle you like that."

She pursed her lips. "The point is, my brother doesn't think I can take care of myself."

"You're a woman and he's trying to watch out for you." He shrugged. "And I can understand why he wants to protect his little sister."

She glared at him. "So you think that because I'm a woman I can't take care of myself either? So tell me, if I wanted to leave right now, would you stop me?"

His jaw twitched. "I shouldn't have to. You should know what's good for you."

"So you'd keep me here against my will?" She tried to step past him but he blocked her way. "You'd overpower me?"

He stepped forward, backing her against the tree. "Why not? That seems to be what you like."

He dragged her into his arms, his lips taking hers in a forceful kiss. She stiffened, resisting the urge to melt against him. But her anger began to disappear when he pulled her tight to him, her breasts crushed against his hard, muscular chest. She longed for him to stroke them, to rip off her shirt and nuzzle the soft skin.

He stroked his hands down her sides to her hips, then pulled her against his body, his hard erection pressing against her soft belly. Oh, God, she wanted to feel that big cock. To hold it in her hands and stroke it. To feel him press it to her opening and glide inside. Deep and hard inside her.

She clenched her thighs as his hard lips dominated and his big body trapped her immobile against the tree. No escape.

She drew in a breath, wanting him so bad she thought she'd die from the need.

His tongue spiked into her mouth, and he rocked his pelvis forward. He was big and hard and she just knew he was going to take her, here and now. Just like Donovan would.

But Donovan hurt her.

She couldn't let this happen.

He grabbed her wrists and pushed them over her head, holding her firm, his big, hard body pinning her to the tree. She pushed against his hold, but he was too strong. Panic rushed through her and she shook her head, breaking the demanding kiss.

"You're going to force me into submission? Just like he did?"

The heat faded from his intense gray eyes, and they hardened into glinting steel.

"Shit." He drew back and released her. "All you had to do was say no."

He turned around and strode away.

She sucked in air as he disappeared through the bushes, her heart pounding.

Oh, God, she had been so aroused being overpowered by him. She had wanted him to take her right here against the tree. But those feelings reminded her of how she'd felt around Donovan when he'd taken control.

And that had terrified her.

But Steele wasn't Donovan. Right from the beginning, he had been protective and caring of her.

And now she'd driven him away.

As she walked back along the path to the house, she heard a bike engine roar to life, then zoom away. When she pushed through the bushes, she saw that Steele's bike was gone.

She spent the day trying to be useful. She made lunch

for everyone while they sat by the lake in front of the house, and after dinner, she helped with the dishes. Steele was still gone as the sunlight faded deep orange over the lake and finally disappeared, leaving the world in darkness.

She played cards with some of the others, but finally decided to go to bed. She heard Steele's bike return some-time after midnight and she held her breath when he came into the house, waiting for him to come upstairs. Wondering what she would say to him.

But he didn't come up.

She was restless and anxious as another hour passed. Then she heard someone on the stairs. She gripped the blanket and watched the door. But then she heard a woman's giggle and the rumbling of a man's voice.

It was Raven and Rip.

She hopped out of bed and pulled on her jeans, then peered out the door to see their bedroom door closing. She raced down the hall and tapped on the door.

It opened and Rip stood there.

"Hi. I . . . uh . . . wanted to ask Raven something."

"Sure. Come in." He stepped aside and she scooted into the room.

Raven walked toward her. "What is it?"

"I wanted to know if you could help me with something?"

Rip grinned. "Can I watch?"

"Rip!" Raven sent him an admonishing stare.

"Sorry, I'm just . . ."

Raven laughed. "Yeah, we all know what you're *just*." She turned to Laurie. "Don't mind him. He's had a few drinks and is ready to go, if you know what I mean. What is it you want?" she asked with a smile.

"Well, it's about Steele. He and I had an argument this morning."

"Yeah, I figured."

"I want to fix things between us, and I thought you could help."

Steele sat on the couch alone in the living room, nursing a beer. Everyone else had gone to bed. He wanted to go up to bed, too, but Laurie was there and he didn't know what to say to her. And if she was asleep, climbing into bed with her just seemed . . . wrong. Especially since she'd accused him of trying to take her against her will.

Fuck, what could he do to prove to the woman she was safe with him?

A door closed upstairs and he could hear quiet footsteps and murmurs on the stairs. Then Raven and Rip entered the living room.

"Oh, Steele, you're still up." Raven stood there, her gorgeous body on display in a scant bikini.

His cock swelled at the sight of her.

Rip stood behind her.

"Steele, don't you think you ought to go up and get some sleep?"

He shook his head. "Not yet."

Raven sat down beside him. "Look, I know you and
Laurie had a fight, but I just looked in on her and she was
sound asleep. Whatever you argued about, you can sort it
out in the morning."

"I have a better idea." He rested his hand on her long,
silky thigh, slowly sliding upward. "Why don't you and I
and Rip enjoy a little together time?"

But she grabbed his wrist just before his fingers brushed
her bikini bottom.

She shook her head. "Afraid not. I'm looking forward
to some alone time with my man."

"Are you sure? Seeing you in that skimpy little bathing suit has made me hard and ready for you."

Raven laughed and stroked over his big bulge. "Oh,
you're hard and ready all right. But that boner is for Laurie, not me. And I'm not taking a backseat."

"I think it would be me taking the backseat," Rip said.
"Steele would be riding up front."

Steele's cock grew harder.

"Yeah? My point is I'm only going to have one rider
tonight." She glanced at Steele. "I'm not here to relieve
your needs, you know."

Steele sucked in a deep breath and nodded. "I know
that. Fuck, I'm sorry, Rave."

She patted his shoulder. "It's okay. Now go to bed."

His eyes narrowed. "Why do you guys want to get rid
of me anyway? You can fuck in your room."

Raven smiled. "Because there's a great hot tub out
on that deck and I want to get naked in it and enjoy the

attention of my man. And it won't be as much fun with you in here mooning around."

He grinned. "I could come out and watch."

"No," she said firmly. "Now go to bed."

"Yes, ma'am."

Steele reluctantly pushed himself to his feet and started up the stairs.

When Steele opened the bedroom door, he was surprised to find the light on. As he stepped into the room, his heart rate jolted when he saw Laurie lying in the bed, her hands above her head in handcuffs. Her shoulders and arms were bare, and he suspected she was totally naked beneath the sheets. His already-hard cock ached.

His chest constricted and he strode toward the bed to release her. Had one of his crew done this because Steele had been out and they assumed nothing had changed?

"I'll find the key and take those handcuffs off."

She gazed at him, her big blue eyes wide. "No, I don't want you to."

Steele stopped in his tracks and frowned. "Why?"

She drew in a deep breath. "Steele, I'm sorry about the things I said earlier. I know I can trust you. I was just . . . reacting. And when you kissed me so forcefully, it reminded me of Donovan and—"

"I'm not like that asshole."

"I know that. I just . . . freaked out. It was a knee-jerk reaction."

"So why the handcuffs?"

"Because I want to show you that I trust you." She sat up a little more and the covers slid down her chest, revealing the swell of her breasts. His cock twitched.

"I was thinking that with me bound like this, I could show you just how submissive I can be."

She wanted him to take her like this? Naked and bound to his bed?

His heart raced.

She had one hand closed in a fist and she opened it now, revealing the key to the handcuffs in her palm. "This is for you. Because I trust you."

He stepped closer. Could he do this? Take her while she was bound in his bed? When he was her protector?

He reached for the key and took it from her hand. At the merest brush of his fingers against her soft skin, he knew he had no choice but to obey the intense craving inside him and finally know the pleasure of gliding deep inside her body. His groin ached at the thought, and his cock swelled even more.

He placed the key in his jeans pocket, wanting this symbol of her willing surrender to him close, not discarded in a drawer. He sat down on the bed beside her and stroked her cheek. He smiled, then leaned toward her and brushed his lips lightly on hers, loving the soft sweetness of her mouth.

But his hands ached to touch her body, to explore the luscious curves hidden from him by only this thin cotton sheet. He wanted to see her naked breasts, and her long, lithe body. And her pussy. Would it be bare? Or decorated with a fringe of hair? Or maybe a pretty shape?

He longed to see. And she'd given him permission to not only see, but to touch. To enjoy.

His tongue glided over her lips. He kissed the corner of her mouth, then nuzzled her neck.

"You are so beautiful."

"Steele, I am totally under your control," she murmured softly. "There's nothing I can do to resist you."

His heart thundered in his chest. She wanted him to dominate her. Despite how her boyfriend had treated her. Or more likely, because of it. She wanted to get past her fear, and she trusted Steele to help her.

He caressed her soft shoulder, then dragged his finger down her chest to the edge of the sheet. Slowly, he peeled it downward, revealing the swell of her round breasts, then lower, until they were totally exposed.

They were so round and pert. Perfect. He cupped one, watching her face as he did. She watched him nervously, but when he closed his hand around her, her eyelids closed and she arched against his hand. He cupped her other breast and squeezed them both gently, delighting in the feel of her hard nipples poking into his palms.

He leaned down and licked one hard nub, then drew it into his mouth and suckled. She moaned softly.

He stood up and pulled off his shirt. She watched him, her gaze drifting down his naked chest, then locking on his hands as he unbuckled his belt. He unfastened the button, then drew down the zipper. Fuck, the intense look of anticipation in her eyes sent his hormones skyrocketing. He dropped his jeans, then stripped off his boxers and tossed them aside. He grasped his big, hard cock and stroked it as he stepped toward her again.

She licked her lips and he couldn't help but take her up on the invitation. He sat beside her, leaning against the headboard and twisted toward her. He stroked her cheek with the tip of his hard cock and she turned her head toward him.

She stared at his erection with such hunger he thought he might explode right then.

"Lick it," he said.

She leaned closer and her soft, wet tongue rasped across his tip. He suppressed a groan at the intense pleasure.

"Now take it in your mouth." The words came out hoarse, revealing his deep need for her.

Her soft lips opened and glided around him. Fuck, her mouth was so warm and sweet as it closed around his big cockhead. His stomach tightened as he controlled his desire to drive into her mouth, then thrust until he came deep in her throat.

She squeezed him inside and he groaned.

"Now suck me."

She obeyed and pleasure washed through him.

"Ah, fuck, baby, that feels so good." He cupped her head, then glided deeper into her mouth.

She gagged a little and he pulled back, but then went forward again. Slower this time. He drew back and forward. Slowly. Going a little deeper each time.

He knew he was too big for most women, and longed to be fully immersed in a woman's mouth, but not here. Not now.

She sucked as he filled her mouth again and again. Heat built within him and he was close.

He knew he should pull out, but he wanted to come in her mouth, and she wanted him to dominate her.

"That's so good, baby." He stroked her hair from her face as he pivoted in and out of her mouth.

He was so close. He groaned. "Oh, yeah. Baby, I'm going to come in your mouth."

She didn't tense. She squeezed and sucked, pulling on him, driving him wild, then he groaned again as red-hot lava pulsed through him and he erupted into her mouth.

She continued to suck as he filled her, then she glided back and licked his tip. Finally, he slipped from her mouth and she smiled up at him.

He stroked her hair, then turned away and stepped off the bed beside her. He grasped the sheet covering her from the waist down and lifted it, drawing it off the end of the bed, revealing her totally naked body.

Her pussy was clean shaven.

Laurie caught her breath as Steele stared at her naked folds. Heat swelled through her and she wanted him to touch her. He pulled her knees wide, exposing more of her to his gaze, then he knelt between her legs. When his big fingers touched her sensitive flesh, she sucked in a breath. He stroked her, then a thick finger slid inside.

"Ah, you are so fucking wet."

He leaned forward and licked the length of her slit, then nuzzled his tongue inside. She could feel her insides melting, adding to the slickness already coating his fingers as he glided his finger deeper.

"Baby, I'm going to make you come, and I want to hear you call out my name when you do."

He slid a second big finger into her and they glided in and out. His mouth found her again and his tongue pushed into the tiny nest of folds covering her clit. Then intense sensations blasted through her as he found it. His tongue glided over it, then he began to suck lightly. She arched against him, wanting to feel more of what he was giving her.

"Do you like that?" he asked as he peered up at her, plunging his fingers deeper.

"Oh, yes."

He thrust them in and out faster as he licked and cajoled her clit. Heat washed through her and pleasure spiked. She arched and moaned as heat consumed her.

"Oh, yes. I'm . . ." She sucked in a breath as blissful sensations vibrated through her. "I'm coming."

He sucked harder, his fingers still stroking inside her.

"Who's making you come, baby?"

"Steele." She gasped. "Oh, God, yes, Steele." Tears streamed from her eyes as the building pleasure burst into pure joy. Her senses expanded and ecstasy swelled through her. She moaned long and loud, riding the wave of complete and utter bliss.

It went on and on. Steele's insistent attention pushing her to the absolute limit.

Finally, she collapsed, gasping for breath.

It had never been like this with Donovan. When he had handcuffed her that first time, he'd forced her to suck him until he was swollen and close to bursting, then he'd climbed on top of her and penetrated without caring if she was ready, then used her for his own pleasure. He gave no regard to the fact he hadn't satisfied her need. Not that she would have come anyway. She hadn't enjoyed anything about his careless, rough treatment.

At the feel of hot, hard flesh against her now, gliding along her slick opening, she stiffened. A whimper escaped her throat at the memory of how it had felt when Donovan had pushed into her, without caring if she was ready or not.

But this was Steele, not Donovan. She was surprised he was ready again, so he'd caught her off guard.

Steele immediately rolled aside. "What is it? Was I hurting you?"

She shook her head. "No. I was just surprised you were hard again."

He smiled. "Of course I'm hard again. Tasting your hot pussy. Feeling you come against my mouth. Fuck, any man would be."

At the stricken look on her face, Steele realized she'd been thinking of a different man. Probably that jackass Donovan, who had treated her so badly.

"You were thinking of him, weren't you?"

She dropped her gaze. "No, you just caught me off guard, that's all."

"It's okay. I won't do anything you don't want me to do. I told you that before."

He stood up and found his jeans, then pulled the key from his pocket and released her from the handcuffs.

"Steele, it's all right. I want you to make love to me." She grasped his wrist. "I want to feel you inside me."

Fuck, the need in her eyes tore at him, and his cock twitched with the same need.

But he couldn't. Not knowing she might be thinking of *him*.

He pulled on his boxers and walked to the other side of the bed, then turned out the light and climbed into bed behind her. "And I want to be inside you. But it's not going to happen tonight."

He turned her away from him and pulled her into his arms, then drew her tight to his body. She wiggled her sexy ass against him and his cock ached.

"Are you sure?" she asked.

He tightened his arm around her waist, trying to stop her arousing movements. "Stop moving," he demanded through gritted teeth. "I'm trying to be a gentleman here."

She stopped and relaxed into his arms. Then she took one of his hands and drew it to her breast, then pressed it to her soft flesh.

"Yes, you are," she said.

They lay in the darkness in silence. His cock ached with

wanting her, but he would will it to relax. Ten minutes later, he was still hard and aching, despite all his concentration. How could he calm his intense desire with her soft breast pressed into his palm, and her warm soft body tight against him?

If she were to make one movement, he was sure he would explode.

This was pure torture, but he wouldn't let her go now for the world.

"Steele?"

"Mmm?" He didn't risk saying anything. His hoarse voice would give away his intense need for her. As if she couldn't feel it pressing hard against her back.

"Thank you."

He sucked in a breath, then kissed the back of her neck. A few moments later, her deep, even breathing told him she was asleep. He lay there for a long time holding her close, until finally his body relaxed and he dropped off to sleep, too.

Laurie woke up in the warmth of Steele's arms. She opened her eyes and thought about last night. It had been incredible. They had each brought the other to orgasm, yet they still had not made love. She shifted and he murmured behind her, still asleep, but she could feel his hard bulge pushing against her backside.

He had been a gentleman, as he had put it. Because she'd had a flashback to how Donovan had treated her, Steele had backed off.

But she wanted Steele so badly. She wanted him inside her. She wanted to share that intimacy with him.

She turned in his arms, then she kissed his raspy neck.

Steele awoke to a raging hard-on and soft breasts crushed against his chest. Laurie's soft hand stroked down his chest as her sweet lips kissed his neck, and under his jaw.

"Fuck, woman," he said sleepily, "you could drive a man to distraction like that."

She laughed. "But I don't intend for you to be distracted at all." She grasped his chin and drew it down until he gazed at her. "I intend for you to be fully focused on what we're about to do."

She wrapped her fingers around his cock, still encased in his boxers. But she squeezed him and he groaned. He flipped her onto her back, then prowled over her, raining kisses on her neck.

"Woman, you'd better learn right now. I'm in charge."

She pursed her lips. "Yes, Steele. Whatever you say."

"That's more like it." He glided his hand down her stomach, then dipped into her soft folds. Slick moisture surrounded his fingertips. "Fuck, you are so ready for me." He drew his cock from the slit in his boxers and slid the tip over her slick folds, loving her murmur of pleasure.

"Oh, baby, I am going to fuck you so hard."

"Yes. Oh, please." She arched against him.

A loud knock sounded at the door.

"Fuck," he muttered, then snapped, "Go away."

He pressed his cockhead to her opening and pushed forward a little.

"Steele, this is important," Rip called from the other side of the door.

"I said fuck off."

She cupped his cheeks, gazing at him with wide, dewy eyes, as he pushed forward, his cockhead slipping into her. Just a little.

The knocking at the door turned into a pounding.

"I'm not kidding, man. You better get out here."

Laurie gazed at the door. "I think he means it."

"Fuck." He kissed her, then pulled back, slipping from her welcoming warmth.

He grabbed his jeans and pulled them on.

"I'll be right back." He stared at her. "Don't move."

She smiled. "Whatever you say."

Steele scowled as he followed Rip down the stairs.

"It's Killer on the phone."

"What the hell does he want?" Steele demanded.

"I'll let him tell you that."

Steele stormed into the living room and picked up the phone.

"Yeah, what is it?" he snapped.

"I just want to warn you that I'll be coming out there to make an arrest. I have no choice."

"You're going to arrest me for kidnapping?"

"No. I'll be arresting the woman for theft."

He tightened his grip on the receiver. "Theft? What the hell are you talking about?"

"Apparently, Donovan Blake has charged that she stole a very expensive diamond necklace. I have no choice but to come and arrest her."

"Thanks for the heads-up."

"You understand I expect you to keep her there until I get there."

"Of course, Officer Grainger. I understand completely."

Steele hung up the phone.

"So what are we going to do?" Rip asked.

Steele locked gazes with him. "We're going to get her the hell out of here."

Wanted

Laurie stretched in the bed, longing for Steele to return, her whole body aching for him. She could still feel his massive cockhead against her intimate flesh and . . . oh, she ached at the thought of it pushing inside her.

She could hear his footsteps on the stairs. Hurrying. Returning to her.

She could hardly wait to feel him slide inside her. Her insides ached with need and she stroked her nipples as she watched the door, waiting for him.

His footsteps hurried along the hardwood floor toward her, then the door burst open.

She smiled and opened her arms to him, but to her surprise, he just scowled.

"You've got to get up. Right now." His harsh, commanding voice tore through her. He grabbed a T-shirt from the small duffel bag on the dresser and pulled it over his head.

Her stomach clenched. "Steele, did I do something wrong?"

"What?" He stared at her, and suddenly seemed to see her. His glittering granite eyes softened. "No, baby. We've just got to get out of here. Fast!"

Her heart raced at his words, filled with the threat of oncoming danger. She pushed the covers aside and sat up, then grabbed her undies from the floor and pulled them on. As she pulled on her bra, she caught him watching her as he stuffed things into his bag, his gaze lingering on her breasts as she tucked them away in the lacy cups.

"Fuck, the timing on this sucks."

"The timing on what, exactly?" she asked as she tugged on the shirt she wore last night, then retrieved her jeans.

"Officer Grainger is on his way over to make an arrest."

Her gaze shot to his. "He's going to arrest you for kidnapping me?"

"No, baby, he's going to arrest *you* for stealing that diamond necklace your jackass boyfriend gave you."

"Donovan? Oh, God. But he gave it to me. I'm sure we can—"

"You can explain it until you're blue in the face, but whose word are they going to take? Yours? Or his?"

She sucked in a deep breath. "He's trying to punish me."

"That's right." He grabbed her hand and drew her out the door with him, his bag in his other hand. "And he might not stop at jail."

Laurie clung to Steele as the bike sped along the highway, her arms snug around his waist, her body pressed tight to his. The rest of Steele's crew had sent them ahead while they finished packing up. Steele had told her they would catch up with them at a predetermined place.

She and Steele had gotten out of the house in less than ten minutes and had been riding for hours, but the feel of his hot, hard body and the vibration between her legs kept her body hot and ready.

In the bedroom, before he'd shocked her with the news that they had to run, they had been so close. His plum-shaped tip had teased her wet opening and had glided inside, however briefly. She squirmed on the seat, aching to feel him inside her.

She tried to ignore it. The adrenaline when they'd fled before the police arrived to arrest her had dwarfed the feelings for a while, but then they'd built up again.

She squeezed him, her aching breasts crushed against his back. She couldn't stand it any longer. She needed to feel him.

She ran her hand over the supple leather of his jacket, caressing his chest, but she couldn't feel *him,* so she slid her hand down and stroked over the front of his jeans. Up and down until she felt a bulge form.

Oh, God, she wanted him inside her. She pulled his zipper down and slipped her hand inside. As she stroked his thickening cock, still under the scant protection of his boxers, his hand grasped her wrist and held her still. Then he drew her hand away. Undeterred, she glided her other hand over his growing erection and slid under the cotton to wrap her fingers around him.

If he really wanted her to stop, he could pull over and

tell her so. She stroked him and he released her other wrist, grabbing the handlebar of the bike again, his fingers clamping tightly around the grips, just like she gripped tightly around his hard shaft.

He shifted on the seat, then she felt the bike turn and he pulled off the highway onto a side road. She squeezed his big member, and drew it from his jeans, then stroked his length.

He veered off the road, then pulled onto the shoulder.

I guess he wants me to stop.

He dismounted the bike, drawing himself free of her hold, his face looking stern as he zipped himself back up. Then to her surprise, he slid her forward and mounted behind her. Suddenly, they were speeding forward again, but with his arm snuggly around her waist, pulling her tight to his body. She could feel his erection pressed against her backside, straining against his pants.

His hand slid up and stroked her breast, then he cupped it and kneaded it in his hand. The wind rushed past her face and she could barely catch her breath. Her nipples, swollen and hard, ached for him. He slid to her other breast and squeezed it, then his fingers traveled down to the hem of her T-shirt and slipped underneath. He cupped her breast again, then tugged down the lace cup to free her nipple. At the feel of his fingertips pinching her sensitive bud, she arched against him, her head resting back against his shoulder.

The wind rushing past her face . . . the bike . . . his touch . . . all left her breathless and aching for more.

He continued to stroke her, alternating from breast to breast. Sometimes cupping and stroking, sometimes teasing her nipples, until her senses were alight with intense desire.

Then he slid down her belly and unzipped her jeans.

Oh, God, his fingers slid inside and underneath her panties until he stroked her slick flesh. She opened her thighs wider and his fingers glided over her. She arched forward as he stroked her slick folds. The feel of his calloused, masculine fingers gliding into her soft, wet passage drove her wild.

Pleasure pulsed through her as he stroked deep inside her, then drew out and touched her clit. She moaned into the wind, then he tweaked and she gasped. He slipped inside her again, this time ignoring her aching clit.

He alternated, gliding deep inside her, and slipping out to tease her swollen button.

She wanted him inside her. She *needed* release.

As if reading her mind, he slowed the bike and pulled off the road. She glanced around and realized they were now on a small dirt road with trees all around. He pulled over and stopped the bike.

"What the fuck are you doing to me, woman?" He pulled off his helmet as he dismounted, then unfastened hers and pulled it off.

Then his mouth was on hers, his tongue driving into her insistently. She opened for him and he filled her, driving deep, exploring her mouth with authority, his hands cupping her face.

Then he drew back and grasped her leg and pulled it over the bike so she was sitting facing him.

"Take off the fucking jeans."

She wiggled them down her hips and he pulled them off her legs. She watched with hunger as he unzipped his pants and pulled out his erection. Then he stepped toward her and pulled aside the crotch of her panties. She moaned at the feel of his hot, hard member against her.

"Fuck, woman, you were driving me to distraction." Then he drove forward, impaling her.

"Oh, God." She clung to him, holding his body tight to hers, then he drew back, the ridge of his cock dragging on her passage, sending tremors through her.

Then he drove deep again and she moaned.

He drove into her again and again, her whimpers building to long steady moans as pleasure swamped her senses.

"Oh, Steele, yes."

He nuzzled her neck as he drove deep again. The feel of his lips heightened her senses and she cried out. Her nerve endings glistened with intense sensations and when he drove into her again, she felt the tidal wave begin.

"Oh, yes." She clung tight to his shoulders. "Steele, I'm . . ." She gasped as pleasure rushed through her. "I'm coming." She wailed, throwing her head back as she shot to heaven, her body exploding in a tumultuous burst of ecstatic bliss.

He groaned as he thrust, then jerked forward, holding her tight against him as he pulsed inside her.

They stood like that for a long moment, ensconced in each other's arms. Finally, he smiled down at her, and kissed her, his hands cupping her cheeks.

"Now we need to get back on the road."

She smiled, feeling more content than she had in . . . forever. "Yes, sir. Whatever you say."

It was getting late in the afternoon and Laurie's stomach was rumbling. Steele had grabbed a handful of granola bars and several bottles of water on the way out of the cabin this morning, but the two bars she'd eaten weren't enough. She wanted dinner and didn't know when or where Steele would stop to get something to eat.

But she knew he would take care of her. She rested her head against his solid back, her arms snug around his waist.

Steele veered off the main road onto another road that disappeared into trees. Soon they turned onto another smaller road and drove for a while. The road split at a Y junction and as Steele continued, after a short time, the gravel road diminished into a dirt road, then soon became a narrower path with clumps of grass studding the surface. He pulled into a clearing and stopped the bike by a big tree, then dismounted.

It was a lovely spot by a small lake, trees surrounding them, giving them lots of privacy, though this far off the paved road there was probably no one around for miles. The sun glittered on the calm surface of the water.

He pulled off his helmet and opened the storage compartment on the back of the bike and tugged out a blanket and spread it on the grass, then handed her a bottle of water. She opened it and took a swig.

He settled down beside her and gazed out over the water.

"This is a nice spot," she said.

He nodded. "We have several places like this across the country where we like to stop when we're in the area. Sort of regular places to camp. This one's well off the beaten track, so it's a good place to go when you don't want to be found."

"Do you often not want to be found?" she asked.

He shrugged. "We're not criminals, if that's what you mean. But I like getting away from it all. I grew up in a city. Crammed into a little box called an apartment. Working all the time. I always wanted to get away. Ride the open road." He sipped his water. "Be free."

"So what stopped you?"

"Commitments. Time. Money."

"What kind of commitments?"

He gazed at her, his expression somber.

"I'm sorry. It's none of my business."

He sighed. "No, it's okay." He capped his water then stretched out on his side, head propped on his hand. "I had a little sister. Chrissy. Our mom . . ." He shrugged. "She took off when I was a teenager, leaving just Chrissy and me to fend for ourselves. I dropped out of school and got a job. Several, actually, while trying to keep Chrissy in school."

"Where is she now?"

His eyes darkened in pain and she instantly regretted asking.

"She died of a drug overdose."

Laurie reached out and placed her hand on Steele's arm. "I'm so sorry."

"She was sixteen, in with the wrong crowd." He shook his head. "I tried to keep her safe, insisted she stop hanging with them, but she wouldn't listen. When I was home, I could keep on top of things, but I often worked nights as a bouncer, so I left her alone too much. Wild Card would look in on her when he could, but"—his hands balled into fists—"fuck, she still managed to get into trouble. I scared the shit out of the guys she dated, to make sure she didn't get pregnant, but . . ." He just shook his head.

She took his hand, her stomach tightening at his obvious pain. "You did the best you could."

"If I'd done my best, she'd still be alive."

She stretched out beside him, facing him, and stroked his cheek. "Sometimes things happen . . . people do things . . . you can't control. It's not your fault."

He pursed his lips and said nothing. She knew he wasn't convinced, and nothing she could say would change his mind. All she could do was be here for him. Listen if he wanted to talk.

Now she understood why he had tried so hard to keep her at the cabin. He couldn't protect his sister, but he would do his best to protect her.

After a few moments of silence, he pushed himself to

a sitting position and stared toward the sun hanging low on the horizon.

"The others should be here soon," he said. "You want to go for a swim?"

She would love to go in the water, especially since she'd had no chance to shower this morning, but she had no bathing suit and really didn't want to be swimming naked with Steele when the others showed up.

Though the idea of swimming naked with Steele was exciting. Of seeing him peel off his T-shirt and reveal that massive tattooed chest of his. And his impressive cock.

A shiver ran through her. She wanted to climb on top of him and ride him to heaven.

But the others would be here soon and she didn't want to be caught in an embarrassing situation.

"I think I'd like to just relax." She gazed at him. "You could go for a swim. I'll watch." She grinned.

He laughed. "I don't know if I should just give you a free show." He leaned down and brushed his lips on hers, then smiled, a gleam in his granite eyes. "Maybe you should entice me to take off my clothes."

He lay down and pulled her in for a deeper kiss. His hand found her breast and he cupped it in his big, warm hand. She leaned into his palm, loving the feel of his big fingers caressing her soft flesh.

"That's nice, but I don't really want to . . . you know . . . get naked when the others might arrive at any time."

He chuckled. "We don't actually have to get naked to fuck. We've already proven that."

He rolled her onto her back and prowled over her, covering her with his big, solid body, his rising erection pressing against her stomach. He tilted his pelvis, grinding his hard shaft against her mound, sending heat humming through her.

Oh, God, it felt so good.

But she pressed her hands on his shoulders and pushed. "No, Steele, I'm really not comfortable with this."

He gazed down at her, then frowned, but he drew back.

"Because the others might show up in an hour?"

"Or earlier. I'd be . . . embarrassed."

He sat up. "If you're going to be my woman and travel with the crew, you'll have to get over that kind of thing."

His woman? Travel with them? Was he serious?

The idea of traveling with Steele was exciting, but could she really live that way?

She'd moved a lot as a kid, with her dad in the army, and she'd always wanted a real home. When her parents had died when she and Craig were still young, they'd gone to live with her grandparents in Jasmineville. She had been about thirteen and found it difficult to make friends in a new town, still suffering from the loss of her parents. She had longed to have friends who knew her, whom she could talk to, share her deepest secrets with. She wanted a stable home, with a network of people who knew and cared about her.

She wanted roots.

She had started to build that dream. She had friends, though none as close as she'd like. She still seemed to keep up barriers, but she was working on that. And she'd bought a town house six months ago. Her own real home.

She was already worried about losing her job—a job with one of Donovan's companies. He could, and probably would, have her fired, and she could forget about getting a good reference for a new employer. Her chest compressed. She had no savings, and without a good job, she didn't know how she would pay the mortgage, but she knew she had to find a way. She would not lose her home.

She frowned. No matter how appealing it might be, she couldn't just take off and ride with Steele and his crew.

Anyway, she'd only met Steele a few days ago. She had no idea if they'd be compatible in the long run. Her common sense told her they wouldn't be. What did she have in common with a tattooed, nomad biker? She liked her stability, and was horribly unsettled by this whole situation.

She sat up and hugged her knees, tipping her head to gaze at him, and decided to ignore his comment about being his woman to delve into a more troubling issue.

"Steele, what do you think is going to happen? About the charges against me, I mean. If they arrest me, won't they put me in jail for a long time? That necklace must have been pretty expensive."

"No one's going to arrest you."

"How do you know that? We can't keep running forever."

He pulled her into his arms and held her close. "Because I won't let them." He kissed the crown of her head with a soft brush of his lips. "I told you. You're my woman."

She sighed. She should probably set him straight, but it felt so good in his arms like this. She felt so protected.

He lay back on the blanket, taking her with him, and she snuggled more deeply into his arms and felt herself dozing off.

Laurie awoke to the roar of engines. She opened her eyes and glanced up to see two men towering over her. She blinked and, in the fading light of the setting sun, she recognized Wild Card and Shock staring down at her.

"You two lovebirds hungry?" Shock asked.

The smell of food tickled her nose. "I'm starving."

She sat up and glanced around. Rip and Raven walked toward them with paper bags from a fast-food restaurant in their hands. Magic spread a blanket beside the one she and Steele were on and the others sat down. Dom pulled containers of fries and wrapped sandwiches from the bags and passed them around.

Laurie unwrapped her burger and bit into it. Shock handed her a bottle of beer, and one to Steele. It was cold. She twisted off the cap and took a sip.

Soon they were all settled on the blankets, enjoying their meal.

"So Shock is an odd name," Laurie said. "Why do they call you that?"

He grinned. "It could be my shockingly large cock."

Steele laughed. "Your shockingly small one, you mean."

Shock snorted. "Not fair comparing me to your be-hemoth."

"Don't listen to him," Dom said. "You may have no-ticed that Shock likes to cook. Well, he used to share a place with Steele, Wild Card, and me, and someone had left behind this old electric griddle and he'd cook pancakes on it every morning. The thing was old and the wiring faulty so he got a shock every time he turned it on. But he insisted on using it every day."

"It had really even heat and browned the pancakes per-fectly," Shock explained defensively.

"So they call you Shock because you got an electrical shock?"

Wild Card laughed. "Yeah, I think it's more because of his resemblance to a housewife rather than a biker dude."

Shock threw a crumpled wrapper at Wild Card's face. "Yeah, you want to take over the cooking?"

Wild Card grinned. "I wouldn't think of it, sweet-heart." Then he puckered up and sent him a kiss.

"And talking about big cocks . . ." Raven said with a grin.

"Were we?" Rip asked. "Or was that just in your mind?"

She laughed and squeezed his knee. "You want to know how this one got the name Rip?" Raven grinned. "He told me it was short for Ripley's Believe It or Not."

Laurie watched as Raven stroked Rip's thigh affection-ately.

"Of course, I assumed it was because . . ." Raven's gaze dropped to his crotch and she grinned. "But it seems that Steele should have gotten *that* name."

"Yeah," Shock said. "What Rip never told you was that he got the name because someone caught him reading the Ripley's book. I think it was to win a bet, but maybe he's just a bookworm."

Raven gazed at Laurie and winked. "Either way, I think I got stuck with the wrong biker."

Rip laughed and pulled her tight to his body. "Baby, I haven't heard you complaining when we're together."

Her eyes glittered in delight. "Well, I do get a taste of Steele's generous member on occasion."

Steele cleared his throat. "And Wild Card. He's just trouble brewing. Just when you think things are going along fine, he'll pull a Card Trick . . . do something totally random . . . to throw everything off."

"Like kidnapping me?" Laurie asked with a smile.

Steele slipped his arm around her and pulled her close. "That was one of his better tricks."

Laurie gazed up at him. "And how did you get your name?"

"You haven't figured that out?" Raven asked.

Laurie stared at her, then at Steele, wondering if she was missing something. Some sexual innuendo? Because he grew hard as steel?

"Doesn't he remind you of someone? Someone famous?"

Laurie stared at his features. "When we first met, I did think he looked a bit familiar, but I couldn't place him."

"Think Remington Steele," Raven said. "Like in the old TV show."

A young Pierce Brosnan flickered into her mind and she realized Steele looked like a very rugged version of him, with his glossy dark hair swept back off his face, his square jaw, and extremely handsome face. "My mom used to watch that show." Laurie smiled. "That's it. That's where I've seen you before."

Steele just rolled his eyes.

"This is fun," Laurie said. "And Magic?"

"Well," Magic said, "that story's a little crude and has to do with the fact that I'm bi. Let's just say, people say I work magic."

"Okay." But Laurie couldn't help wondering what he meant specifically. Maybe he would tell her sometime. She turned to Dom. "And you, Dom?"

Was it because he was a Dominant? She'd seen him command Raven. And Magic.

Dom laughed. "My name is Dom."

Laurie nodded. "I know."

"No, I mean my name is Dominic. Dom for short. The fact that I like to order people around is just a happy co-incidence."

"And me . . ." Raven pointed at her head of long, glossy black hair. "Raven hair."

Steele stroked his hand along Laurie's hip. "We'll be keeping an eye on what ride name to give you, so keep that in mind."

Because she was his woman and he assumed she'd be riding with them, a thought that warmed her heart, and at the same time, sent dread through her, because she knew at some point she'd have to set him straight.

"What about Tempest?" she asked, just because she liked the sound of it.

"You can't pick your own ride name," Rip said. "We pick it for you."

Raven winked. "So be careful you don't do anything embarrassing, or they'll pick a name to forever remind you of it."

They finished their food. As they cleared everything away, Wild Card and Magic started a fire, then they all sat around it and had a few more beers.

"So how did you all get together?" Laurie asked.

"Steele and I go way back." Wild Card was laying on the other blanket they'd spread out and leaned back on his elbows. The breeze stirred his spiky blond hair. "We met Dom on a construction site we were working one time and the three of us hit it off. Started sharing a house together."

"The one with the shocky griddle?" she asked with a grin.

"Yeah, that thing was in there for a year before Shock showed up and started using it."

"Him we met in a bar fight," Dom chimed in. "He was new in town and being a bit belligerent and five guys jumped him." Dom shrugged. "We thought we'd even out the odds."

"I was holding my own," Shock said.

Steele laughed. "Yeah, sure you were."

"And Magic?" Laurie asked.

Wild Card plucked a bright yellow dandelion flower and twirled the stem between his fingers. "Oh, one day on the road we went out drinking and the next day, Dom just showed up with him. He's been with us ever since."

"Sort of like Rip showed up with me?" Raven smiled.

Dom and Magic were sitting cross-legged, side-by-side, and Dom put his arm around Magic's neck and pulled him close with a chuckle. "Yeah, a lot like that. But he came with his own bike."

Laurie sipped her beer. She loved the camaraderie between these men. And the easy acceptance of the intimate relationship Dom and Magic obviously shared.

"You said you were all in a house. Where is it?" she asked. "Do you all live there now?"

If they were just traveling around temporarily, maybe Steele would be amenable to the idea of settling down. Could she convince him to come and live in Jasmineville? Her house could easily accommodate the two of them.

She knew it was probably a crazy idea. Steele didn't want to leave his crew, but if he was open to the idea of moving, maybe they could figure something out.

"No, that place is back in Chicago," Shock said. "We've been on the road for a year now, and don't plan on stopping anytime soon."

"Steele and I always talked about hitting the open road," Wild Card said, "but we had to earn a living. Then Shock came along and changed all that."

"Really?" She gazed at Shock.

"His family's got money." Magic took a swig of his beer. The thorny tattoo around his wrist, designed to look like sharp thorns were tearing into his flesh and making it bleed, still disturbed her. "He doesn't like to talk about it, but he's got access to funds and doesn't mind sharing."

"Don't get us wrong," Steele added. "We don't live in the lap of luxury, but Shock covers the basics. We live simple."

Laurie's hopes of settling down with Steele came crashing down. He'd always wanted to be a drifter, and she wanted roots.

It was getting cool and she shivered. Steele noticed and slid his arm around her. She leaned into his warm, solid body.

"I think it's time to turn in," Steele said.

Rip stood up and walked to his bike, then opened the compartment on the back. He tossed Steele two sleeping bags. "We stopped and got one for Laurie, too."

"Good thinking." Steele unrolled the two bags, but zipped them together to make a double. He pulled back one side and climbed in, then patted beside him.

Laurie glanced around a little self-consciously, but noticed Raven climbing into a sleeping bag with Rip. Laurie slid in beside Steele and he wrapped his arms around her, pulling her close to his hard, muscular body. And his thick, hardening cock. She stiffened, but he rubbed her shoulders with his big hands.

"Don't worry about it," he murmured against her ear.

She relaxed a little and lay there under the stars, fully conscious of the fact a whole gang of bikers and one biker chick lay in sleeping bags around her, and their leader's arms were around her. And his cock was big and hard from wanting her.

Crickets chirped loudly and she saw the odd firefly flare in the darkness, but despite Steele's big erection pressed tight against her, sparking her desire, she finally slipped into a deep sleep.

Laurie awoke to Steele's big hand cupping her breast, holding her close to his body. She murmured her approval and smiled, opening her eyes to the bright sunshine. To see grass close to her face, and Magic and Shock sitting drinking coffee a couple of yards away.

Oh, God, she was turned on and so was Steele, from the feel of his hard shaft against her backside. He squeezed her breast.

"Steele," she murmured.

"Mmm. Yeah, baby?"

He was just waking up. Probably not yet aware of their surroundings.

"Time to wake up."

"Believe me, I'm awake." He pressed his cock tighter to her butt.

"Steele, everyone can see us."

He chuckled and pulled her onto her back, then prowled over her, trapping her beneath his body.

"Don't worry about them," he said, a glint in his eye

as he stared down at her, then he took her lips posses-
sively.

"Yeah, just carry on. Don't mind us," Shock said.

Heat flashed across her cheeks. She pressed her hands
to Steele's chest, struggling a little, panic blasting though
her. He released her lips, but didn't move away.

"I told you, you need to get over this shyness."

"But I can't . . . not in front of them."

"Then let's go somewhere private."

She sucked in a breath. It didn't matter. The others
would know what they were doing.

"Don't worry about it," Magic said. "We're going with
Raven for a swim." He winked. "We'll be too busy to no-
tice what you two are doing."

Steele rolled onto his back, then unzipped the bag and
sat up. So did Laurie. Raven and Rip were already at the
water's edge and the others were joining them. Raven
stripped off her T-shirt and dropped her jeans, then stood
there looking sexy and gorgeous in her bra and very skimpy
panties.

"Bitch, kneel down and suck my cock," Dom commanded.

Raven tipped up her chin. "Who's going to make me?"

Shock stepped behind her and grabbed her arms. "I
will, then you'll suck me next." He urged her toward Dom
and pushed her to her knees. She stroked over Dom's jeans,
then unzipped and pulled out his big cock. She smiled at
his erection, then wrapped her lips around it and glided
down.

He closed his eyes. "Ah, fuck, that's what I want."

Laurie felt need rising in her. Raven was so relaxed and accepting of her role in this group. She certainly seemed to enjoy it, and despite the fact Dom and the others seemed to be dominating her, it was clear that she was the one who was truly in control.

"I don't feel right watching them," Laurie murmured to Steele by her side, but she couldn't drag her gaze from the scene in front of her. Raven had serviced Dom for a bit, and now she was working on Shock. Rip had shed his pants—they all had—and stroked his cock while he watched his woman pleasure another man.

God, Raven had kidded that she was with the wrong biker because of how big Steele was, but Rip was nearly as big. In fact, none of these men were slouches when it came to their endowments.

"They don't mind. And I think it's turning you on as much as it is me." Steele drew her onto his lap and stroked her hip, then his hand glided over her crotch.

She arched against him.

He grinned. "I knew it. Why don't we join them?"

She gazed up at him. "You would really let those other men touch me?"

"Touch you. *Fuck* you. Yeah, the very thought turns me on so much I could come right now."

"But how could you want that?"

He tipped up her chin and gazed into her eyes. "I trust these men with my life. I share everything with them, and they with me."

"So your woman is just a piece of property to be passed around?"

He frowned. "No, baby. It's not like that. When I have something truly wonderful, like Rip has with Raven, I want to share with them. I want them to experience the joy I have." He shook his head. "But don't for a minute think that means any more than sharing a physical experience. Because you are my woman and they all know that. Just like they know who Raven belongs to. And who belongs to her."

Steele pulled her into a deep kiss. "You're mine. And nothing and no one is going to change that."

She stared at him, dumbfounded. She should say something. Set him straight.

But she liked the possessive look in his eyes. Directed at her. Despite the fact he was willing to share her, it was clear he wouldn't give her up to anyone.

It gave her a surge of joy. And confidence.

She knew she could actually walk over to the naked men only thirty yards away and strip down to nothing, then let them touch her and fuck her, and Steele wouldn't be jealous. Yet she knew there would be dire consequences if anyone hurt her in any way.

To be cared for like that intrigued her. And made her feel like there was somewhere she belonged.

Steele knew he was pushing Laurie hard, but he was hoping to break her out of her narrow view of what a sexual relationship could be. If she couldn't accept being shared by his crew, he could live with that, but he knew he'd have to push her boundaries to see what she would be willing to do.

She could always say no, and he would be fine with that.

"Steele, do you have a beach towel?"

He gazed down at her. "Sure. Is this an idle question or do you want me to get it for you?"

"Yes, please."

He pushed himself to his feet and approached his bike, wondering what was on her mind. Maybe she'd worked up the nerve to go swimming in her bra and panties. He pulled the towel out of his duffel bag in the storage compartment.

When he turned around, his eyes popped as he saw Laurie standing on the sleeping bag, facing him, totally naked.

She held out her hand and he stepped toward her and gave her the towel. Of the others, only Shock noticed Laurie's nudity and his gaze traveled the length of her, but he could only see her from the back. He didn't have the glorious view Steele did of her luscious round breasts, and her pretty little pussy atop delightfully long, shapely legs.

Laurie wrapped the towel around herself and walked toward the water. "Are you coming?" she asked.

As he watched her delightful ass sway as she walked, his cock twitched. "Very nearly."

She laughed as he moved into step beside her. She took his hand, but as they got closer to the others, she squeezed his fingers and slowed down.

"Steele, I'm a little nervous."

Fuck! He wanted her to do this, but he didn't want her to feel she had no choice.

"Look, babe, you don't have to do anything you don't want to do."

"No, it's not that. The thought of doing this is really exciting, but . . ." She gazed down at their joined hands. "It would be easier if you just took control. I'll do whatever you want me to do."

Fuck. That meant he had to reel in what might happen because he had to anticipate her discomfort.

"I have an idea. Your safe word is 'sparrow.' That will stop everything and allow us to regroup. But you can use the word 'parrot' if you're not comfortable with something that is happening, so I can shift what's going on. That way I can push your limits without being worried I'm going too far, because we both know you can slow things down, or change direction if you're not comfortable. Okay?"

She smiled timidly at him. "Perfect."

She glanced toward Raven, who was sitting on a tree trunk moaning as Rip licked and sucked her pussy. The men were gathered around watching her, the ones who hadn't come yet stroking their cocks. Laurie watched and waited, her cheeks flushing as Raven gasped and wailed her release.

Rip leaned back, a smug look on his handsome face. Laurie stepped forward and waited until all of the men glanced her way. Once she had their full attention, she gazed at Steele and he nodded, then she dropped the towel.

All the men stared at her magnificent naked body. Wild Card's jaw dropped.

"Men, I want to introduce you to Laurie. I'm making her available to you for your enjoyment." He gazed at her, delighted by her prettily blushing cheeks. "Isn't that right, Laurie?"

"Yes, sir."

For a split second, he wondered if he could go through with this. He had only felt her sweet pussy around him once. A part of him wanted to sweep her away and take his fill of her, again and again, until he was satisfied before he shared her.

But he knew he would never be satisfied.

He would never get tired of touching her. Kissing her. Fucking her.

Damn, who was he kidding? *Making love* to her.

"Wild Card, you obviously want to touch her," Steele said. "Do it."

"What?" Wild Card's wide eyes turned to Steele, then a grin spread across his face. "Yes, sir."

Steele watched his friend walk toward Laurie. He had swirls of blue, purple, and red tattooed the full length of his left arm, with three two-inch stars left blank. He'd gotten it not long after Chrissy had died, and Steele suspected the stars represented Wild Card, Chrissy, and him.

Wild Card had been his friend for a long time and there was no one he would rather share his woman with.

Wild Card ran his fingers through his spiky blond hair as he walked toward Laurie, a huge grin on his face, then he stood in front of her, smiling down at her.

"Damn, I've wanted to do this ever since I first saw you." He ran his finger from her shoulder to the swell of her breast, then he cupped her lovely mound of flesh.

She drew in a breath as he caressed her. He found her other breast and caressed both at the same time.

Steele's cock pressed hard against his jeans, begging to be released from the tight confines.

Laurie felt strange and embarrassed standing there naked in front of the men, but Wild Card's big hands on her breasts and his gentle caresses had her blood pressure rising. It brought back memories of being on the bike with him after he'd kidnapped her. She'd been filled with adrenaline then, and she was now, too. His big cock had pressed against her, but despite the fear that had flooded her then, she had known deep inside he wouldn't hurt her.

He had saved her from Donovan. He'd protected her.

And now he was touching her with gentle strokes.

"Wild Card, kiss her. And Shock. You stand behind her."

"You bet." Shock walked toward her.

Wild Card cupped her face and lowered his lips to hers. His tongue stroked her mouth and she opened to allow him in. Shock stepped close behind her. His hard, hot body pressed close against her and he wrapped his hands around her hips and pulled her tight to him. She could feel his hard cock against her back. As he pressed tighter to her, she felt Wild Card's erection pressing against her belly. Her insides heated with need.

Shock's hand glided up to her waist, then along the sides of her breasts. Wild Card drew his face from hers, his hazel eyes dark as he stared at her with desire. Shock's hands covered her breasts and he caressed her.

Wild Card leaned down and Laurie felt him move one of Shock's hands out of the way, then her breath caught as he took her hard nipple in his mouth.

"Hey, Steele, we want to try the new woman, too," Magic said as he and Dom stepped beside her, watching.

"I'll help as you're waiting your turn," Raven offered as she walked toward Magic. She crouched in front of him and wrapped her hand around his hard cock.

Laurie watched the big shaft glide in and out of Raven's mouth as delightful sensations rocked through her at the feel of Wild Card's tongue teasing her sensitive nipple. Shock moved in front of her and took her other nipple in his mouth and she moaned in appreciation.

Rip stepped behind Raven. "Stand up, baby."

She stood, Magic's cock in her hand, then bent over, exposing her behind, then began to suck Magic again. Rip stroked her round behind, then slid his finger into her slick folds. Raven slid from Magic's cock, holding it in her hand and turned her head to gaze back at him.

"Rip, you know I'm loving that, but you can have me anytime."

He smiled. "Okay."

Rip moved away from Raven, then stepped behind

Laurie and grasped her hips and pulled her back to him, just like Shock had done. His thick shaft pressing against her was bigger than Shock's. She was getting so hot, she wanted a cock inside her, but could she really go through with this? How many of them would actually fuck her?

All of them, a voice in her head begged, shocking her socks off.

Rip drew her backward. After a few steps, he sat down on a large, fallen tree trunk, pulling her onto his lap. Shock and Wild Card followed and both knelt in front of her and captured her nipples again. Shock began to suck, making her moan, as Wild Card's lips brushed down her stomach. He stared at her folds, then pushed her knees wide. His finger pressed into her dampness and he stroked her slit. She sucked in air as pleasure pounded through her.

"Very pretty." Wild Card glided his fingertip through her folds again, then slowly pushed a finger inside her.

Panic welled through her and her gaze shot to Steele, who sat on a rock and watched her, his big cock in his hand.

She felt guilty enjoying the attentions of the men, but seeing how turned on it made Steele reassured her.

She heard muffled moaning and glanced beside her to see Dom thrusting into Raven from behind while she continued to suck Magic. She pulled his cock free of her mouth periodically to suck in air.

"Oh, yeah, baby. I'm close." Magic groaned as Raven took him deep.

Laurie contracted around Wild Card's finger as she watched Raven bob up and down on Magic while Dom

thrust into her faster and faster. Wild Card leaned forward
and his tongue lapped between her folds. Laurie's eyelids
fell closed as heat surged through her. Beside her, Magic
grunted, then a moment later, Raven moaned loudly.

Oh, God, Laurie wanted a man inside her, too.

"You are so sweet, baby," Wild Card said when he
came up for air.

"Let me taste." Shock pressed his face to her dampness and his tongue pushed inside her.

Rip covered both her breasts and kneaded them in his
palms. Wild Card stood up and wrapped his hand around
his cock.

He stepped closer and offered his big shaft. She licked
her lips and glanced at Steele again, who was stroking his
enormous erection. She wrapped her lips around Wild Card
and took his cockhead into her mouth. She squeezed and
sucked him while he stroked her hair back from her face.

"Sweetheart, that feels so good," Wild Card said.

Heat swelled inside her as Shock found her clit and
teased it. Then he sucked and her pulse rocketed upward.
Pleasure exploded inside her and her head fell back, her
mouth dropping the cock in her mouth. Wild Card
groaned, then erupted, the stream of white fluid spurting
upward, then drizzling down his shaft.

She felt Shock's blunt tip press against her and he pushed
forward, impaling her in one deep stroke. He drew back
and thrust into her again, pushing her against Rip's solid
body behind her. Shock pounded into her and she groaned,
then began to moan as another orgasm claimed her. His

big cock kept moving inside her, extending her pleasure, until he groaned his own release.

Shock leaned forward and kissed her, then stood up, his spent cock dropping free.

Laurie leaned back against Rip's muscular chest, catching her breath, which was hard with his big hands still caressing her breasts.

"Laurie, I want to see you between Rip and Magic," said Steele. "I want to see both their cocks driving into you at the same time."

She stared at Steele, not quite comprehending, her head still spinning from the divine pleasure she'd just experienced.

"Both?" she stammered.

He raised an eyebrow. "Is that a problem?"

What was the word? Parrot?

She could stop this anytime she wanted. She drew in a deep breath.

"No problem, sir."

She stood up and as she turned to Rip, she saw that Raven was sucking Magic's cock, making him hard again for Laurie. Raven slipped from the shaft and winked up at Laurie, then she sat down on the grass to watch.

Rip, who was standing now, took Laurie's hand and drew her close to him, then kissed her. His lips moved on hers with passion and his tongue dipped inside her. Her tongue tangled with his as his hands cupped her bottom and he pulled her close.

"Bend over, Laurie," Steele commanded.

As she obeyed, Rip guided her to rest her hands on

the trunk he had been sitting on. She leaned forward and Magic stepped behind her. He cupped her ass and stroked.

"What a sweet view." Magic pressed his cock to her slickness and slowly glided inside her. After a couple of strokes, he drew out and pressed his cockhead to her back opening.

She stiffened a little and he stroked her hip. "You okay?"

She drew in a deep breath and nodded. Donovan had been rough when he'd taken her this way, but Magic's voice was reassuring and his hand was gentle, which relaxed her. Rip stroked her shoulders as Magic eased forward slowly, pushing into her tight canal, stretching her around him. She relaxed into the steady pressure, then sighed when his cockhead was fully immersed.

Rip cupped her hanging breast and kneaded as Magic started moving deeper. Rip tweaked her nipple and she moaned. Magic pushed all the way in. Her canal hugged him tightly and they both stayed still while she got used to him being inside her. Rip teased her other nipple and she moaned.

Slowly, Magic drew her to a standing position. Rip shed his pants, then held his stiff cock in his hand. Magic guided her forward then turned her. The tree trunk was higher here, so he leaned against it. Rip stepped in front of her and pressed his cock to her opening, gliding over her slick slit.

Then Rip's cock slid into her, too. Once he was fully immersed, she sucked in a deep breath. She couldn't believe these two big men were inside her at the same time.

She tightened around Rip, and he groaned.

"Ah, fuck, baby. That feels so good," Rip said. He kissed her then smiled. "You ready?"

She glanced at Steele again, and felt the heat of his gaze, desire glowing in his eyes, and she nodded.

"Okay." Rip drew her into a kiss, moving his mouth on hers passionately as he drew back, then thrust into her.

His big, thick cock stretched her as it moved in and out, sending her pulse skyrocketing. Behind her, Magic began to move, finding a rhythm with Rip, and soon the two of them were thrusting into her, driving her pleasure higher and higher. She clung to Rip's shoulders and began to moan. It felt so good, these cocks thrusting in and out.

She dropped her head back onto Magic's shoulder as an electric blast of sensation quivered through her, then she wailed, pleasure pummeling her in a wash of ecstasy. The men continued to pump, then they both drove forward, trapping her between their bodies, as a long note of joy crooned from her throat. She felt their cocks pulse inside her as they both groaned.

Her knees started to give way and Magic pulled her back against him, wrapping his arms around her waist.

"You okay, sweetheart?" Rip asked.

She gazed at him and nodded as she rested against Magic's solid body.

"That was just . . . incredible," she said.

Rip laughed and Magic nuzzled her neck.

"For me, too, beautiful," Magic murmured in her ear.

Rip grasped her waist and lifted her, setting her on the tree trunk. When he stepped away, she realized Steele was standing beside him.

She smiled when she saw him and opened her arms. He stepped into her embrace and kissed her, his tongue gliding into her mouth.

"Oh, God, I want you, baby," he murmured against her ear. "Room for one more?"

"Always." She opened her thighs and he pressed his big cock to her opening.

He stretched her as he slid inside, since his massive cock was still bigger than any man's there. He began to thrust, slowly at first, then picking up speed. Still in the afterglow of orgasm, pleasure swelled in her quickly.

She wrapped her legs around his waist, allowing him to go deeper, driving her pleasure higher and higher.

"Fuck, baby, I. Love. Being. Inside. You," he said, each word punctuated by a thrust.

"Oh, God, Steele, I . . ." Then she gasped and wailed in the most intense orgasm yet, thrusting her to the stars.

He drove deeper still and pulsed inside her, then she felt his hot liquid filling her. She moaned, delirious with pleasure.

He held her close as her heartbeat pounded against his chest, her rapid breathing slowly returning to normal.

"Oh, God, Steele. I've never experienced anything like that," she murmured.

He tightened his arms around her. "Being with multiple men, you mean?"

She drew back and gazed up at him. "That *was* incredible . . . But I mean being with you. The way you make me feel is . . ." She shook her head, at a total loss for words.

He grinned and claimed her lips again. When he released her mouth, he held her tight to him.

"And I'm going to keep on making you feel that way."

Laurie glanced around nervously as she got off Steele's bike and handed him her helmet.

"Are you sure it's a good idea for us to stop at a restaurant? I *am* a fugitive."

He put his arm around her waist and pulled her close to him as they walked to the door of the diner. "We've put a lot of miles behind us. I doubt they'll be looking this far." He squeezed her. "It's an expensive necklace, but it's not a big enough crime to warrant a huge dragnet to find you."

Shock held the door open for her and she went into the diner, then followed the others to a roomy booth in the back corner. She slumped onto the cushioned bench seat.

Laurie loved riding the big bike, her arms around Steele the whole time, but it was good to relax for a bit.

Lunch came quickly and they all ate heartily. She was about halfway through her sandwich when she felt a prickle, as if someone was watching her. She glanced toward the counter and froze. A policeman was sitting on a stool gazing in their direction.

Her stomach dropped and she glanced away quickly. *Oh, God. Oh, God. Oh, God.*

He'd spotted her. The way he'd been staring their way . . . he must know.

"What's wrong?" Magic, who sat on one side of her, asked.

She stared firmly at her plate. "There's a policeman over there. He's watching me."

"Okay, just relax. We'll figure something out."

She glanced up again and noticed the cop was drinking his coffee, still gazing in their direction with a stern expression.

Laurie wanted to push her plate away—her appetite had abandoned her completely—but she didn't want to do anything to attract his attention. She nibbled at her food, her stomach coiling in turmoil.

"It's okay. He's gone," Magic murmured to her.

Her gaze darted to the stool where he'd been sitting and relief flooded through her. Thank heavens.

"I need to go to the ladies room," she said to Magic, since he'd have to get up to let her out of the booth.

He moved out of her way and she stood up on shaky legs, then hurried to the restroom, needing a bit of space so she could breathe. She had to cross the length of the restaurant and head down a short hallway. Once inside, she stared at her pale face in the mirror, knowing she wasn't cut out for this kind of thing. She'd be a nervous wreck in no time.

She washed her face, then patted it dry and sighed. Soon they'd be back on the road and Steele would lead them somewhere isolated and safe to spend the night again. Steele would look out for her.

She pushed open the door to the bathroom and walked down the hall. Seeing the policeman had shaken her, but she'd been worried about nothing. She stepped from the hallway to the main part of the restaurant.

"Excuse me, miss. May I have a word?"

She almost jumped at the sight of the policemen standing in her path.

His eyes narrowed. "Are you okay, miss? You seem awfully nervous."

She swallowed and willed herself to stay calm. "Yes, officer, I'm fine. Why did you want to talk to me?"

"I noticed you sitting with those bikers. You looked nervous, so I just wanted to make sure that there's nothing wrong. They're not"—he hesitated—"forcing you to be in their company, are they?"

The irony of his statement almost made her laugh.

"No, officer, they're friends."

He nodded. "Fine. Then please pass on a message to your friends. We don't want any trouble here. Okay?"

She stared at his stern expression and nodded. "Yes, sir. I'll tell them."

Then she hurried away.

Laurie held on tight to Steele as they sped along the road. Her heart was still pounding from her encounter with the policeman, but Steele assured her everything would be all right.

A few hours later, they pulled off the main road and set up camp in another isolated area by a lake. She was tired, and when she finally climbed into the sleeping bag with Steele, she fell asleep immediately.

But when she awoke, it was still early. Only the first hint of sunlight brightened the sky. Steele's arms were around her and his breathing was deep and even. She lay in the darkness, trying to go back to sleep, but couldn't. Finally, she slipped from the sleeping bag and the warmth of Steele's arms, and walked toward the water. Soft moonlight reflected on the water with a luminescent glow. She sat on a rock by the water and stared up at the fading stars.

"Can't sleep?"

She glanced around at the sound of Wild Card's voice.

"No, and I don't know why because I'm really tired," she said, keeping her voice low so she wouldn't wake the others.

He sat down on the big rock beside her. "It's understandable. You've probably never had the police looking for you." He grinned. "Unless there's something you're not telling us."

She laughed. "No, this is a first for me. As is riding with a gang of bikers."

"And sleeping with the leader."

She nodded. "And he keeps saying I'm his woman." Her gaze darted to Wild Card's face. She shouldn't have let that slip out.

"And that bothers you."

She shrugged. "Steele is great, and I really appreciate him looking out for me. But I hardly know him."

"You'll never meet a better man."

His frank gaze and the intensity of his words reached inside her and squeezed.

"Has he told you about his sister?"

"A little bit. I know she died of a drug overdose."

"True."

She saw the haunted look in Wild Card's eyes and realized that it wasn't just Steele who suffered from the death of the young woman.

"He was totally devoted to her. He put everything he had into taking care of her," he continued. "And when she died . . ."

He stared down at his hands.

"He hit the bottle pretty hard, blaming himself for her death. And I made the whole thing worse. Before it happened, I'd been trying to help. Get some money together so the three of us could move away from Chicago. Get a new start somewhere. So I started gambling. Figured I'd hit a big jackpot and save the day."

He shrugged. "Of course that didn't happen. I'd gotten in way over my head and one day, about a month after Chrissy's death, some guys came by to collect some of my debts. I got beat up pretty bad. When Steele got the story out of me, he insisted I straighten up or he'd beat me to death himself. He stopped getting drunk and threw himself into working and helping me pay off the rest of my debts."

He gestured to Steele, still asleep on the ground. "That man always has my back. Same with every one of his crew." He locked gazes with her. "If you let him, that man will protect you and take care of you to the best of his abilities. And believe me, that's saying something."

She nodded, knowing it was true. And she loved Wild Card's loyalty to Steele.

"I'm know you're right, but . . . I can't just give up my life and start riding around from place to place. I need more stability than that. I get that it works for Steele and the rest of you, but it's just not me."

Wild Card nodded and leaned back, then he broke the serious mood with a grin. "I could start to think you don't like us."

She put her hand on his.

"Of course I like you. All of you." She squeezed his hand. "And I really appreciate you stepping in when Donovan . . . you know, in the parking garage."

He took her hand in his. "There's no way I could have done otherwise. I wouldn't let that jackass hurt you."

She smiled tremulously. "I know. And thank you."

He kissed her hand. "You're welcome."

Her gaze dropped to their joined hands, and all the tumultuous emotions that had been roiling around inside her swelled to the surface. Tears prickled at her eyes.

"Oh, Wild Card, what am I going to do? My life is falling apart. The police are after me. My ex-boyfriend wants to hurt me." And a crazy biker gang leader thought she was his woman.

And she was starting to believe it.

He wiped an errant tear from her eye, then pulled her into his arms. "It's all right, sweetheart. We won't let anything happen to you."

He held her tight for a few moments, then he looked down at her. She met his reassuring gaze.

"You're going to be all right."

At the warmth in his hazel eyes, and the sincerity in his voice, she believed him.

Then suddenly Wild Card was jarred away from her. Stunned, she realized Steele had dragged him to his feet.

"Keep your fucking hands off my woman." Then Steele's hard fist connected with Wild Card's jaw, knocking him to the ground.

"Steele, I wasn't—" Wild Card stammered.

"Shut the fuck up."

Laurie lurched to her feet. "Steele, what are you doing?" she demanded.

He turned to her, his eyes flashing. "No one touches my woman."

Her stomach tightened and anger welled up in her. "I'm not your woman!"

This was crazy. His protectiveness had turned to possessiveness, which didn't even make any sense given that he'd happily shared her with Wild Card and the others only hours ago.

He glared at her with an angry, possessive look in his eyes—the same one she'd seen in Donovan's too many times—and her anger turned to fear. She jerked back a step.

The storm in his eyes froze for a brief moment while her heart pounded several beats, then he scowled and turned on his heel and strode away. The others were all awake now, watching what was playing out between them. Steele mounted his bike and the engine roared to life, then he sped off down the road and disappeared through the trees.

Laurie's heart still pounded as she helped the others gather their things and pack them up.

"Are we really going to leave without Steele?" Laurie asked as they finished up.

"When Steele's in a mood, he could be gone for hours," Shock said. "He knows we won't wait for him."

"But . . . how will we find him?"

Raven patted her arm. "Don't worry. He'll find us."

Shock handed Laurie a helmet he produced from his bike storage.

"You'd better ride with me," Rip said.

Laurie glanced at Raven in surprise, and she nodded.

"I'm the only man here he will believe won't steal you," Rip explained with a shrug.

Raven smiled and patted Laurie's arm. "And if he does worry about it, I'll set him straight."

Raven walked with Laurie to Rip's big bike.

"I just don't understand why he got so upset." Laurie felt sick at the memory of Steele's powerful fist connecting with Wild Card's face. "Even if we were doing something, which we weren't, after yesterday . . ." She stared at Raven, bewildered.

"I know." Raven nodded and took the helmet from Laurie's hands, then slid it on Laurie's head. Raven smiled as she fastened the helmet for her, like a sister taking care of her own. "He's a guy and they have a strange way of viewing the world sometimes. Rip doesn't mind if I go one-on-one with the others, but that's because he knows I'm well and truly his." She finished doing up the helmet strap and patted Laurie's shoulder. "Steele is unsure of you." Her smile faded a little. "And I assume he has reason to be. You don't really want to ride with us, do you?"

"It's not that. I like all of you, but this life . . . it's not for me."

"Are you sure?" Raven asked.

Laurie nodded. "I moved around a lot as a kid and that was hard on me. Every time I made friends, I was torn away to a new place. Then when my parents died . . ." She drew in a deep breath, fighting back the remembered pain. "I've always wanted a stable place to live. Somewhere to call home. I have that now. My own place. I need that." She shrugged. "And . . . I don't even know Steele. Not really."

And what had just happened with Wild Card proved that.

"We've got to get moving," Rip said as he mounted the bike.

Laurie climbed on the bike behind Rip and slid her arms around his big torso, feeling awkward and self-conscious. It was crazy because this man had driven his cock into her yesterday and sent her into a screaming orgasm, yet she felt awkward sitting on the back of his bike pressed close to him.

Raven climbed on with Wild Card and all the bikes roared to life. Laurie tightened her hold on Rip and the bike lurched forward. Soon they were on the open road, the wind streaming across her face.

Steele sped along the road, adrenaline blazing through him. He took comfort in the feel of the bike beneath him and the miles blurring by.

Fuck, he couldn't believe he had actually hit Wild Card. It was inexcusable to do that to one of his own men. One of his brothers. But the fury at seeing the intimacy between him and Laurie had torn through him, ripping away every shred of common sense.

All he'd known was, he couldn't allow Wild Card to touch her.

But now he was haunted by the stricken look of horror in Laurie's eyes. The fear he'd seen in those blue depths had speared through his heart.

At that moment, she had been afraid of him, and he found that thought unbearable.

Fuck, he would never hurt her. How could she believe otherwise?

But he knew why. The answer was all too clear. It was all because of that bastard she'd been with before.

His heart ached at the thought that she might never come to fully trust Steele.

He'd been an idiot to slug Wild Card—it had been inexcusable. Wild Card was loyal. He would never steal anything of Steele's. But common sense and logic had fled when he'd seen Laurie in his arms, her blue eyes soft and misty as she'd gazed up at him. In that moment, she had looked open and vulnerable to Wild Card, as if she would share her deepest secrets with him, and a wild, uncontrollable jealousy had flared through Steele.

Fuck, he was his own worst enemy sometimes. If Laurie now feared him just like she feared that Donovan bastard, how would he ever recover her trust?

How would he ever convince her to stay with him?

Because he would be lost without her.

He'd never allowed himself a real relationship with a woman. When he'd lived with his sister, Chrissy, he'd been focused on her welfare. And he wouldn't have brought a woman around the apartment with her there anyway. Then, after she'd died . . . he'd erected barriers. He hadn't wanted to open his heart to someone and risk that kind of pain again. But Laurie had caught him off guard. Protecting her had opened him up to that kind of concern again. He liked caring about her. Being open to her.

She was like a potent drug. Now that she was in his system, he would never give her up.

His gut clenched. In that way, was he really any different from her ex?

Laurie dipped her fry in the pool of ketchup on her hamburger wrapper and took a bite. Normally, she didn't eat French fries, but nothing about her life was normal now, so why should her eating habits be? A little indulgence couldn't hurt.

"Don't worry," Raven said, eyeing her over her own

burger. "We'll catch up with Steele and you two will sort things out."

Laurie pursed her lips as Rip set down his tray of food and sat beside Raven at the outdoor tables at the fast-food restaurant. Wild Card sat beside Laurie and the other men settled at the table beside them.

"How did you two get your food so fast?" Wild Card asked.

Shock laughed. "All they had to do was bat their eyelashes and the lineup parted."

Raven grinned. "Or maybe it was my badass attitude."

Shock snorted. "Honey, your ass is a lot of things, but bad ain't one of them."

Rip laughed. "I actually think that guy let you in so he could stare at your sexy little asses while you ordered."

Laurie's cheeks flushed at the comment. The two men who had let them go ahead in the restaurant lineup *had* shown a keen interest in their backsides. And when Raven had slipped off her black leather jacket while the clerk had pulled together their food order, Laurie had glanced around and noticed that the men's hot stares had settled on Raven's T-shirt, specifically where it stretched tight across her generous bosom.

"Rip, you don't mind when men stare at Raven that way?" Laurie asked.

Rip shrugged. "She's a beautiful woman. If I got bent out of shape every time a man admired her, I'd be a mess."

He pointed a fry at her. "But if a guy touches her, I'd flatten him on the spot."

"Except for the five men you ride with."

"That's right. Do you really think that's so strange? Especially now that you've experienced it yourself."

She sighed. "It's just that, with what happened this morning, maybe it's not as simple as you all seem to think. Clearly, Steele isn't as comfortable with sharing as he thought."

"There are reasons," Rip said. "Ones that are up to him to share, or not."

"Okay, but let me ask you this. If a new man joined the gang, you'd be okay with him having sex with Raven?"

Rip's lips compressed. "No one new's joining the club."

"We'd have to know a guy really well . . . totally trust him," Dom said, "before we'd let him in. He would have had to prove himself."

"So you wouldn't let me in?" Laurie glanced around.

"Of course we'd let you in."

Laurie raised an eyebrow. "Why? How have I proven myself?"

Raven smiled. "Oh, hon, by the way you make Steele feel. That man's clearly in love with you." She reached out and took Laurie's hand. "We're all hoping you'll wind up joining us, because we love Steele."

Rip smiled. "And, Laurie, let me assure you, emphatically, that even as a new member of the crew, if you want to have sex with Raven," his eyes glittered, "I absolutely approve."

Raven laughed as she released Laurie's hand, but the lingering feeling of her warm touch sent a shiver through Laurie. She knew all men fantasized about watching two women have sex, but . . . was he actually serious?

As Laurie took a sip of her drink, she was highly aware of the men staring at her speculatively.

Rip took a sip of his soda, then reached into his jeans pocket and pulled out his cell phone. Raven had told Laurie that there was one cell phone in the group. Generally, they didn't care about communicating with people outside the crew, but having one just made sense.

She wished that Steele had been carrying the phone. Then they could have contacted him. As Rip checked his messages and texts, she hoped there was one from Steele.

Rip held the phone to his ear and listened, and his gaze shifted to Laurie, a serious expression on his face. Laurie's stomach clenched.

Was it bad news? Had something happened to Steele? Or did he just not want her around anymore?

Rip put down the phone. "That was Killer. He said that if you bring in the necklace, your ex will drop the charges."

Laurie locked gazes with Rip, hope flaring through her. Could it really be that easy? Drop off the necklace and she would be free? She'd get her life back?

"But he says the offer ends at ten o'clock tonight."

"That's crazy. We'll never get back to Marin Falls in time," Raven exclaimed.

"We might have if I'd checked messages sooner." Rip frowned. "It's been sitting on the phone since yesterday."

Raven stroked his sleeve. "Don't blame yourself. The guy had to know it would take time for Killer to get in touch with you. He's playing mind games."

Rip dialed the phone. "Killer? Yeah, I got the message. Look, there's no way we can get back there by the dead-line." Rip glanced at Laurie. "Yeah?"

The conversation went on and Rip mentioned the small town they'd passed through a couple of hours ago. After a few minutes, he ended the call.

"Killer thinks he can work something out. He's going to call us back."

"Could he be doing this to keep us here?" Laurie asked, anxiety quivering through her. "Now that he knows where we are, he could be sending someone to pick me up."

"I trust Killer with my life," Rip said. "And yours."

Laurie nodded. The phone rang and Rip picked it up.

"Yeah." His gaze locked on Laurie. "Really? But that's gotta be a five-hour ride from here." His hands clenched into fists. "Yeah, I get it. *His* terms." He listened for a while, clearly getting detailed instructions from his friend. "Okay. I'll make sure I get her there in time."

He stuffed his phone into his jeans pocket and turned to Laurie.

"Okay, we'll have to boot it to get there in time. Lau-rie, you have to take the necklace to an Officer Parker, someone Killer knows and trusts. Your ex says if Parker confirms he has the necklace by ten P.M., he'll drop the charges. And if we don't make it, he'll prosecute and demand the maximum sentence."

Laurie's chest constricted. And with his connections and money, he'd get what he wanted.

"Don't look so worried, Laurie. If we leave now, we should be able to make it with time to spare."

Raven stood up and pulled on her jacket.

"Laurie, where's the necklace now?" Rip asked.

Laurie's gaze darted to his, and her stomach tightened. "I . . . gave it to Steele."

Crossroads

Laurie's heart pounded. They didn't even know where Steele was and with the deadline of 10:00 P.M., they didn't have time to find him.

"Shit, it'd take us at least four hours to get to the next location we agreed on." Rip glanced at his watch. "There's no way we'd make the ten o'clock deadline."

"All we can do is start in the direction of the sheriff's office and hope that Steele contacts us," Wild Card chimed in.

"You know he won't do that until we're plenty late showing up," Dom said. "Which will be too late."

Laurie trembled. They couldn't give up on the opportunity for her to walk away from this mess, but what could they do without the necklace?

"Hey, guys," Shock said. "You looking for this."

Laurie's gaze darted to Shock, who had just returned from the washroom, and hanging from his big fingers was the glittering collar of diamonds in question.

"You've got it!" Laurie exclaimed.

"Yeah, after you gave it to Steele that first day, he gave it to me for safekeeping."

Raven held out her hand and took it, then admired it in the sunlight, an expression of awe on her face. "It's so beautiful."

She handed it back to Shock and he wrapped it in a black-and-white bandana and shoved it in his jacket pocket.

"Let's get moving," Shock said.

The wind raced across Laurie's face as she clung to Rip as they sped along the dark highway. The sun had set and the road was lit by the light of the bikes' headlights and the soft moonlight. They had been riding for four hours straight.

She held tight to Rip, finding comfort in leaning against his broad back. These men really were amazing. It seemed they would do whatever they could to help and protect her. And it had all started with Wild Card snatching her from Donovan's clutches.

She'd never had friends like this. Friends who understood her, and would do anything to help her. In fact, this was just what she'd always wanted. She felt cared for and happy when she was with them.

She rested her head against his back and closed her eyes. She was tired. This whole thing was exhausting, but hopefully it would soon be over. She wasn't cut out to be a fugitive.

After a while, the bike slowed and they pulled off the

highway. Laurie opened her eyes and watched the road ahead. Soon they drove into an urban area. Rip drove along the built-up streets, then turned his bike into the parking lot of an all-night diner.

The other bikers pulled up beside him. Rip dismounted and so did Laurie.

"I'm going to take you over to the police station alone. Having a gang of bikers ride through town is likely to make the cops nervous. Killer suggested you go in alone, so I'm going to wait in a diner near the station while you deliver the necklace." He glanced at her outfit and frowned, then glanced at Raven. "Rave, do you have something that looks a bit less biker babe?"

Raven pursed her lips. "Not really."

Laurie stared up at him, her stomach tightening.

"It's okay," he assured her. "It's not really a problem. We'll just have you lose the jacket before you go in."

"Okay." But she didn't feel better.

Shock handed Rip the crumpled bandana and he tucked it in his jacket.

"You can all wait here and have something to eat," Rip said. "We shouldn't be long."

Laurie and Rip mounted his bike again. He started it up and she clung to him as they rode a couple of miles farther into town. Rip pulled up to the side of the road and stopped the bike in front of a coffee shop.

"Okay, I don't want to hang around outside the police station, and this is the closest place to wait. The station is that building over there." Rip pointed to a brown brick building down the road a bit. "That's the back of it. You'll have to go around the block to get to the entrance. I'll wait right here." He pointed to the coffee shop.

She slipped off the leather jacket and handed it to him, then he pulled the necklace from his pocket, still in the black-and-white bandana, and pressed it into her hand.

"Okay?"

She took the necklace and slipped it into her jeans pocket. "I'm nervous. I keep thinking this is some trick Donovan is pulling. That once I get in there, they'll arrest me."

He tipped up her chin and captured her gaze with his. His midnight blue eyes were reassuring. "You'll be okay. Killer trusts this Officer Parker and his instincts are good. I'm just being extra cautious. No point making them nervous having you show up with a badass biker type."

She nodded.

"Don't identify yourself to anyone until you talk to Parker. Understand?"

She nodded again, then turned and walked along the sidewalk, her legs shaky. It was night, but the road was well lit by the streetlights. A black car drove by, then turned right at the traffic light on the corner. Once it was past, she crossed the street and continued down the street to the corner, then turned, walking out of sight of the coffee shop where Rip sat.

Her stomach fluttering, she walked along the sidewalk. This was a smaller street and no one was around, so she picked up her pace. The car she'd seen earlier was parked along the side of the road. She had an uneasy feeling. She was carrying a very expensive necklace. What if whoever was in the car intended to rob her?

But she realized no one would have any idea what she had in her pocket. And whoever had parked the car was probably already gone in the time it took her to walk the length of the previous street. Still, she hurried past the car, until she reached the next corner and turned right. She could see the entrance to the police station ahead.

She walked up the steps to the door, then drew in a deep breath, trying to calm her nerves. She steeled herself and grabbed the handle, then pulled open the big, glass door and stepped inside.

She walked through the quiet lobby wondering where to go. A uniformed officer walked toward her.

"May I help you?" he asked.

"I'm here to talk to Officer Parker."

"This way." He led her through a door and they walked past a few doorways then he led her into a small meeting room. "Wait here."

She sat in the room wondering if this was an interrogation room, but it looked like a simple meeting room with a table with six chairs around it. There was no big mirror on the wall like she'd come to expect from Hollywood.

"Laurie?" A good-looking uniformed man, tall with wavy blond hair, stepped into the room. He had kind, brown eyes and a reassuring smile.

"Yes."

"I'm Officer Parker." He sat down across from her and pulled a leather wallet from his pocket and showed her his badge identifying him as Officer Glen Parker. "From what Officer Grainger told me, you've been through quite an ordeal."

She nodded. "That's true, and I really appreciate your help." She pulled the necklace from the inside pocket of her jacket and placed it on the table. "Here it is."

He unwrapped the bandana and peered at the necklace, then whistled.

"Nice." He glanced at the clock on the wall.

She peered at it, too. There was barely a half hour left on the deadline.

"Okay. Let's get this done right now," he said.

He laid his badge on the table and placed the necklace in a glittering band below it, then pulled a cell phone from his pocket and took a picture. He tapped on the screen, then she heard the telltale *whoosh* of the message being sent.

"Good, now that's taken care of. Feel better now?"

"I don't know. None of this seems real," she said. "I swear he gave me the necklace. I can't believe he reported it stolen."

"Well, it's all water under the bridge now. You're free to go." He smiled. "Would I say that if I didn't know the charges are dropped?"

She drew in a deep breath and released it. Donovan had put her through hell, and all to have the last word in their relationship, to show her who was in control. Well, he'd gotten his petty revenge, and she was happy to wash her hands of him.

"Thank you so much." She offered her hand and he shook it.

"My pleasure to help." He stood up and she followed him back to the lobby. "Are you okay getting back to your friends?"

"Yes, thank you. Someone is waiting for me in the coffee shop around the corner."

He smiled. "Good. I'll let Officer Grainger know that everything's taken care of."

She stepped into the warm night air, feeling as if a weight had been lifted from her shoulders. Surely Donovan was done with her now and she could return home and resume her normal life. She trotted down the stairs and turned left.

Not that life could ever be totally normal again after these experiences. She was glad to put Donovan behind her, but what about Steele? He had become jealous and possessive this morning, and had taken off. They clearly had some issues to work out.

She turned the corner onto the quiet street, walking with a lilt to her steps, despite the concerns washing through her about Steele.

Vaguely she was aware of the same black car parked along the road that she'd seen earlier. As she got close to it, anxious to get back to Rip and get on with finding Steele, she cautiously stayed a couple of yards from it. Suddenly, she noticed a quick movement in the shadows between the buildings and a big hand covered her mouth and pulled her against a strong body. She struggled for air with the big palm clamped tightly over her, partially covering her nose. She tried desperately to scream, but couldn't. She was shoved forward and the back door of the vehicle opened, then she was forced inside. She was feeling weak from lack of air, and her heart pounded wildly with the adrenaline surging through her.

The door slammed and the car lurched forward.

Steele paced back and forth at the isolated place where they were to camp that night. He was still burning with guilt at having hit Wild Card. That should never have happened. Wild Card was a trusted friend. He was one of Steele's crew.

Fuck, he and Wild Card shared women all the time. It was just sex. It didn't mean anything.

Steele had crossed a line.

Fuck, even if Wild Card and Laurie had had sex right there on the rock, he shouldn't care.

His fists clenched. But he fucking did!

He still couldn't get that soft, vulnerable look on Laurie's face out of his mind. The way she'd gazed at Wild Card. The way she obviously trusted him. Had probably confided in him.

They'd just seemed so . . . close. And it was tearing him up inside. Especially since he felt her holding back from him.

Right now, though, with the crew over two hours later

than he'd expected, he had other things to worry about. What had happened to them?

He grabbed the blanket from the ground and bundled it away, then mounted his bike and drove down the road. Twenty minutes later, he pulled into a parking lot in the local town where he'd seen a pay phone. He dialed Rip's cell.

"Yeah?" Rip said on the other end of the line.

"Where the hell are you?" Steele demanded.

"Steele, fuck. You have no idea what's been going on. I'm in a place called Whitehall, about three hours from where we were supposed to meet you, and Laurie is in the police station."

Steele's chest compressed. "She's been arrested?"

"No, Killer contacted us to say Donovan would drop the charges if she brought the necklace in."

Steele listened with clenched fists as Rip explained about the deadline and the location to bring in the necklace.

"I don't like it. It seems like some kind of trap."

"Killer wouldn't set us up like that. He's a loyal friend."

"I trust Killer," Steele said. "It's Donovan I don't trust."

"Relax. Killer suggested Whitehall because he has someone there he knows and trusts."

"I won't relax until Laurie is back with us. You said she's in there now? How long?"

"About forty-five minutes."

"Shit. That's a long time to just drop off a fucking necklace." Steele's heart was pounding. "You gonna go in there and find out what the hell is going on?"

"Steele, it could easily take that long. They need to file their report, and it takes time to ensure that gets handled and everything is in order."

"Which means the guy could have changed his mind and she could be sitting in jail right now."

"I don't believe that," Rip said firmly. "Killer wouldn't have offered this deal if he didn't think he could pull it off."

Anger and frustration rumbled through Steele. He felt helpless and that's not a feeling he embraced.

"I'm getting on the road right now. If she isn't out of there in ten minutes, then take the crew and get in there. Take down the walls if you have to but fucking get her out. I do not want that sadistic son of a bitch to get his hands on her again."

"Steele," Rip said in a calm, steady voice, "we are not going to break her out of a police station. If she is in jail, which I'm sure she's not, then we'll find another way to get her out. In the meantime, I'll get on the phone to Killer and find out what's going on. I promise you, I'll make sure she's safe."

"You had fucking better," Steele snarled, then hung up.

Rip dialed Killer's number.

"Grainger."

"Killer, it's Rip."

"Hey, calling to thank me, are you? I bet you're glad that's over with."

"Yeah, I will be as soon as Laurie gets back here. That's why I'm calling."

"What the hell do you mean when she gets back there? Isn't she with you now?"

"No, and she's been in there for close to an hour. I was wondering if you knew—"

"Rip, Officer Parker contacted me over half an hour ago to tell me everything was set. She'd already left."

Rip tightened his grip on the phone, his gut clenching. "Oh, shit."

Steele was going to kill him. But worse, if anything happened to Laurie, especially after she'd put her trust in him, he'd never forgive himself.

Laurie stared at the back of the driver's head as the car she was in sped through the night. Neither the driver nor the big man beside her, wearing jeans and a black knit cap, had said anything to her since they'd pulled her into the car. The man in the hat had held her mouth covered for ten minutes or more, his thick arm around her waist holding her pinned to his wiry, but strong body. Any movement she'd made had triggered him to tighten his hold, and she'd had to fight off unconsciousness, until finally she'd just rested against him. Clearly, he hadn't wanted her screaming while they drove through the town.

Once they'd reached the highway, he'd finally released her and she'd scooted as far away from him as she could get in the limits of the backseat. Now she sat there, sucking in air while they drove.

She didn't know how much time had passed and she wondered where they were taking her.

"Pull over," the man beside her said to the driver.

"Why?"

"Don't argue with me. Just do it."

A few minutes later, the car slowed down and pulled off the highway at a rest stop. She didn't know why they were stopping, but maybe she could get out of the car. It was late and there wasn't a lot of traffic, but if she could make her way back to the road maybe she could flag someone down. Or slip into the bushes and hide.

The car stopped in the parking area, away from the lights. There were no other cars to be seen.

In a sudden movement, the man beside her grabbed her by the hips and slid her toward him, then shoved her back on the seat. She panicked as she saw him unfasten his jeans.

"What the fuck are you doing?" the driver asked.

"What the fuck do you think I'm doing? He said he didn't care what shape she was in when we brought her there. If he doesn't mind us roughing her up, then I see no reason we can't fuck her."

Laurie trembled, her heart racing. She tried to scramble across the seat, but he grabbed her shirt and a handful of her hair and pulled her back, then jammed his forearm across her chest, pressing down so hard she could hardly breathe.

"If you don't want to get hurt," he said with a snarl, "then fucking lie still."

He climbed over her, pinning her between his knees and pressing one hand flat on her chest, holding her tight to the seat while he groped her breast with the other. She panicked, flailing and arching wildly, trying to throw him off, but he was too strong. He struck her hard across the face. Pain washed through her as she stared at him in a daze. Then he grabbed her shirt and shoved it up.

"Fuck, man. We got trouble," the driver said.

The man on top of her glanced out the window. "What are those fucking bikers doing here?"

"Maybe they know we've got her."

Hope flashed through her. Had Rip figured out the people in the black car had kidnapped her and he'd pursued them?

"Or it's just a coincidence and they're taking a break. This is the only rest stop for the next thirty miles."

"Well, I'm not fucking taking a chance." The driver started the car and backed up, then pulled onto the road.

One of Laurie's arms was pinned between her body and the man's knee, but she flung the other arm up, trying to reach the door handle, hoping to swing it open. Her captor grabbed her arm, squeezing it painfully.

He glared at her, his cold eyes pure evil. "Lie still or I will beat the crap out of you."

She sucked in a breath and laid there, suffering knowing Rip and the others were only yards away, but they couldn't help her. Because they didn't even know she was here.

"I'm not stopping again," the driver said. "I don't want

trouble with those motherfuckers, so just keep it in your pants, and let's get rid of her as soon as possible."

"Fuck, whatever." He released her, and sneered as she sat up. "And, bitch, we're not that stupid. The safety lock is on. You wouldn't've been able to get their attention back there."

She sat up and leaned against the door, as far from him as she could get. She didn't even fasten her seat belt. That small safety measure would force her closer to him. She'd rather die horribly in a car accident than be an inch closer to him than she had to be.

They drove for what seemed like forever. Finally, they pulled off the highway and soon traveled along a long, winding road. Eventually, they pulled up to a big cedar house.

Her eyes widened when she saw it illuminated in the moonlight.

She recognized this house from the pictures she'd seen of Donovan's several county houses he'd shown her one time.

Oh, God. Donovan was probably in there waiting for her.

The man in the hat opened the car door, grabbed her arm, and dragged her from the car, then shoved her toward the house.

The driver stepped beside her and both men took an arm and hurried her along the stone path to the front steps, then to the entrance. They knocked on the door. A moment later it opened, and she found herself staring at a leering Donovan.

He stepped aside while the two men dragged her into the house. He closed the door and followed. Past the spacious foyer was a large living area with sleek, minimalistic furniture, expensive-looking and somewhat at odds with the idea of a rustic country home. But her gaze locked on the large cage in the center of the room.

Large was relative. It was about six feet tall, but was only big enough to allow one person the barest amount of space. She glanced at Donovan and the dark gleam in his eye confirmed exactly what she feared. Her gaze returned to the cage, eyeing the stainless steel bars. He intended to put her in there. Before or after he beat her . . . or worse . . . she didn't know.

"Do you have the necklace?" he asked calmly.

Her gaze darted back to him. "I gave it to Officer Parker."

"Yes, of course." He walked toward her.

The other two men each still had firm grips on her upper arms so she couldn't move away from him as he glided an unwelcome finger along her cheek. She suppressed her urge to flinch, not wanting to give him the satisfaction.

"A shame. It was such a pretty collar." He walked to a table along the wall and opened a drawer. "Now you'll just have to settle for this."

He stepped toward her with a thick, black leather collar in his hand. It had a sturdy, round, steel ring on the front and two D rings on each side. She tried to pull her arms free from his henchmen's grips, but they squeezed tighter until she was sure they'd left her bruised. She winced as their fingers dug into the flesh of her arms.

"You know you never should have walked away from me." Donovan pushed her hair to one side and wrapped the thick, stiff collar around her neck, pulling it uncomfortably tight, then fastened the buckle at the back.

The coarse leather abraded her skin, and she felt a little panicky with it so tight, as if she would choke, but she knew better than to complain. If she did, he would probably tighten it even more.

"Did you enjoy your time as a biker slut?" He picked up a strand of her hair and toyed with it. "Did you service all of them?"

Her cheeks heated as she realized she couldn't even deny his insinuation, not that it would matter if she had.

The other two men stared at her, almost drooling. Would Donovan give her to them and watch, just as he had tried to give her to Wild Card in the parking garage? Anxiety quivered through her.

Donovan stepped in front of her then nodded to the two men, who released her.

"Take off your clothes," he commanded.

She drew in a deep breath, frozen to the spot.

She wasn't just going to strip in front of him and his two men. Even though she knew he wouldn't stand for her disobeying him. She stared at him, immobile, her heart pounding.

He stepped toward her and she tried to step back, then the men grabbed her arms.

He pulled something from his pocket and flicked it and she realized it was a pocketknife. He grabbed the hem of her shirt and cut through the fabric, then he ripped open the front of the shirt, exposing her heaving breasts, covered only by the black lace cups of her bra.

One of the men pulled the torn shirt down her forearms and twisted the dangling garment behind her, binding her arms as she struggled. With the two men restraining her, Donovan unfastened her jeans, then tugged them down, despite her kicking and twisting. She fell off balance and they let her fall to the floor, dropping down beside her. She'd worked her arms free from the torn shirt, but they grabbed them now and held them immobile. Donovan pulled her jeans off and tossed them aside. He knelt over her, a knee on either side of her thighs, and stared down at her, an evil smile on his face.

"You should have stripped when I told you to," he said, then he flicked open his knife again.

He tucked one of his fingers under her bra strap, his touch sending anxious tremors through her, then he flicked the blade. She winced at the cutting pain as he nicked her skin with the tip while slicing the strap.

"How unfortunate." His eyes glittered as he dragged his finger over her cut, then raised it, blood beading on the tip. "I seem to have cut you." He licked the drops from his finger, then stared at her again.

In a quick motion, he slashed her other strap, maliciously cutting her again. She lay there staring up at him, sucking in breaths of air, willing herself not to move. His fingers slid under the band of her bra at the side, then a sick feeling quivered through her at the sharp sensation of another nick.

He wouldn't hold back this time. He would do whatever he wanted with her, probably even kill her, then just dump her body somewhere and nobody would be the wiser.

Because she knew that no one knew he had her. Steele would not be able to find her here.

Oh, God, she might never see Steele again. Right at this moment, all she could think about was seeing his face again. Feeling his strong, protective arms around her. All her doubts about leaving her home to ride with Steele evaporated. At this moment of clarity, she knew that all she really wanted was to be with Steele. Forever.

But now that seemed impossible. She really didn't think she'd survive this night.

Donovan tossed aside her bra and leered down at her. The other men's gazes also locked on her bare breasts. She felt sick inside.

Donovan roughly fondled one breast.

"Now let's see that juicy little cunt of yours." Then before she could catch a breath, he slashed both sides of her panties, nicking her twice more.

He leaned forward and grasped her wrists. His two henchmen released their hold on her as Donovan pinned her hands over her head, his gaze locking on hers.

"There's a black shoebox on the couch," he said to one of the men, still staring into her eyes, looking smug at the fear he must have seen there. "Get it and put the shoes on her."

The men moved away and within moments she felt one grasp her ankle and force her foot into a tight-fitting, very high-heeled shoe.

"I know how you like your stilettos." His lips turned up in a malicious smile. In fact, he knew she hated them.

She felt hands fastening them around her ankles. She wanted to kick and wound with them, but the strong hands prevented her from doing that. Donovan strapped leather bands around her wrists, then stood up and the other men grabbed her arms and lifted her to her feet. She steadied herself on the extremely high, narrow heels, almost tumbling to the floor again. She glanced down to look at the shoes, which had to be seven-inch heels, with an inch-high platform under the sole.

'Well, don't you look like the perfect, sexy slut." Donovan's hand cupped her bare bottom.

She couldn't help herself. She lifted her foot and jabbed the sharp end of the heel into his shoe-covered foot.

"Fuck!" He lurched back, knocking her off balance, but his henchmen stopped her from falling. Sparks flared from Donovan's cold, gray eyes. He grabbed her arm and tugged her toward him, then smacked her hard across her face. She fell to the ground in a daze, her jaw aching.

"Bitch! You'll regret that." His blazing glare shifted to the men. "Put her in the cage."

They pulled her to her feet and marched her to the tall narrow cell. One rough hand brushed over her breast, squeezing it, and she stifled a cry. Donovan would probably just encourage the man if she made any protest. They reached the cage and the wiry man ran his hand over her ass as the driver opened the door.

"Before we put her in . . ." the wiry one said, "uh . . . you said you didn't care if we touched her."

"You want to fuck her?" Donovan raised an eyebrow, watching the rising fear in her eyes. "Right here in front of me?"

"I don't give a shit where." The wiry man gave her breast a rough squeeze. "I just want to hear the bitch scream."

"Oh, she'll be screaming all right, but not from your rough handling." Donovan's gaze locked on her face, taking in her flaming cheeks and rapid, anxious breathing. "I wouldn't mind watching you and your friend fucking her at the same time while she screams in protest." He grinned evilly. "Or in pleasure, the slut she is."

The wiry man stared at her with cruel, heated eyes and started to unfasten his pants.

"But not tonight." Donovan walked toward the cage. "I don't feel like sampling another man's—I should say men's—sloppy seconds. Put her in the cage."

The wiry man scowled and pushed her inside.

"Fasten her wrists." Donovan watched while the wiry man grabbed her left wrist and held it to her side, then the driver used a metal clip to fasten the ring on the wrist strap to the cage. She tried to fight them while they grabbed her other wrist and attached it at her other side, but all she accomplished was bruising herself as her struggles battered her against the cold metal bars.

Now she stood precariously balanced on these ridiculous shoes, her arms restrained at her sides.

"Use this to secure her legs." Donovan handed the driver two black cords. "You can attach it around the heels."

The wiry man grabbed one of her ankles and pulled it to the side, and the driver tied the heel of her shoe to the bar. When he grabbed her other ankle and pushed her legs as wide as the narrow cage would allow, she lost her balance and her ankle twisted painfully. She cried out in pain. The wiry man grabbed her hips, then stood up and pushed her against the cage, his body holding her firm. The feel of him against her sent her skin crawling. His hands roamed over her body.

Donovan simply watched for a few seconds, then finally said, "Get on with it. Tie her ankle."

The wiry man sank back down and pressed her foot back so that the driver could tie the shoe to the cage. He stood up, his fingers trailing up her thigh. Revulsion jolted through her at his rough touch.

Then he left the cage and the driver closed the door, both men leering at her naked body.

Donovan strolled toward the cage, another thick black cord in his hand. He stepped behind her and tugged her hair to one side, then pushed his fingers through the bars and threaded the cord through the ring on the side of her collar. She pushed aside the panicky impulse to fight him. It wouldn't get her anywhere. He pulled the cord around the bars, then threaded it though the ring on the other side of her collar.

He pulled the cord snug, tugging her head tight against the bars, making her gasp. Then he tied it.

"You two, get lost. I'll contact you if I need you."

The wiry man scowled, then ran his gaze over her naked body one more time before following the driver to the door. When the door closed, Donovan stepped closer behind her. She could feel his breath on the back of her neck.

"So, now we have a little alone time." His fingers slipped through the bars and he coiled her hair around his fingers. "Have you missed me?"

She refused to play these games.

"What do you want, Donovan?"

He laughed. "What do you think I want?"

Her stomach turned as she felt his hand touch her ribs, then stroke along the side of her breast. It slid downward, then curved over her hip. He pulled her tight to the cage while his fingers slid toward her sex.

She couldn't bear the thought of him touching her there so she did the only thing she could think of. Slammed her head back against the bars, startling him.

He growled and tugged her hair, pulling her head hard against the cage, then tightened his hand around her throat and squeezed until she started to black out.

Finally, he released her and she gasped for breath.

"If you do something like that again, I'll punish you by fucking you hard in the ass. Thrusting deep into you. All while you are in that cage. Helpless."

She said nothing. Just tried to quell the revulsion filling her.

All she wanted was to get out of this cage. Her legs were aching balancing on these crazy shoes, especially with her favoring her sore ankle. Having to angle her back so she kept her neck tight against the cage made it all the worse.

With the collar bound tight to the bars, she felt like she was choking.

Donovan walked to the front of the cage and stared at her, his gaze traveling the length of her body.

"But it's late now. I don't feel like putting that much effort into it." He sat down on an easy chair and pulled out his hard cock, then stroked it. He stared at her widened thighs, his gaze locked on her intimate parts. She felt so vulnerable.

His hand moved up and down his erect shaft, his hard gaze on her.

"Are you frightened, slut?"

She refused to answer him.

"Don't worry, I can see it in your eyes." He stroked faster. "I can do anything I want to you." He laughed. "I can beat you. I can make you scream." He groaned. "I can make you beg me to fuck you." He stiffened, then his cock erupted with a stream of white fluid.

He leaned back in the chair, an unsettling smile on his face. Then he stood up.

"I'm tired. I'll see you in the morning."

Disgusted and horrified, she watched him walk across the room. When he reached the hallway, he turned out the light, leaving her in complete darkness.

Oh, God, he was going to leave her standing here in the cage all night?

Her legs were aching already, especially with most of her weight on her right leg because of her twisted ankle. She wished she could sink to the floor and just curl up on the bottom of the cage, but with the tight collar around her neck, she could barely move. If her legs gave out on her . . . Oh, God, she had to fight back tears.

"What do you mean you don't fucking know where she is?" Steele demanded.

Steele had called Rip a half hour after the previous call for an update.

"I've got Killer looking into it, and he's calling her brother to see if he might have any ideas."

"That bastard. Donovan must have got his hands on her."

"Why don't you stay where you are and call me back in twenty? I might have found out something by then."

Steele grumbled his agreement.

"We'll find her," Rip said.

"We had fucking better." Steele slammed down the phone.

He grabbed a coffee at an all-night diner. After twenty minutes, he put a coin in the pay phone and dialed Rip's cell.

"Good news," Rip said. "It looks like we have a lead.

We called his secretary and claimed to have urgent news about a sick relative. She said that he was at a country home for the weekend, though she wasn't sure which one. The closest one is about two hours from here. Odds are, he took her to that one."

Steele's heart raced. "Okay, that's where we'll start. Let's get moving. I'll meet you there."

It was the longest couple of hours of Steele's life as he drove, his gut clenched tight, to meet his crew. He couldn't stop imagining that asshole Donovan Blake with Laurie. Mauling her. Hurting her. *Fucking* her.

God damn it. He drove faster than he should and took chances he shouldn't that night as he raced through the darkness, knowing somehow he would find his woman and save her.

And probably kill the bastard who had hurt her.

The fingers around her neck tightened . . . and tightened . . . squeezing the life from her.

Laurie awoke with a start, the collar so tight around her neck she could barely breathe. She pushed herself straight on aching legs and leaned her head back against the bars again.

"I was wondering if you would wake up this time."

Her gaze darted to the armchair in front of the cage at Donovan's voice. He sat there, quite relaxed, gazing at her. The sky outside the windows was lightening with the rising sun. She had been in this cage for hours now.

"Please let me out of here." Her voice was hoarse. She

didn't want to ask him for anything, an admission she was at his mercy, but she didn't know how much longer she could take this.

"And what will you do for me if I free you?"

"What do you want me to do?"

"Well, for starters, call me Mr. Blake."

"Yes, Mr. Blake."

"Now tell me how sorry you are for being such an ungrateful bitch and running off on me. And how much you would like me to punish you to make amends."

Her legs ached, her muscles straining to balance her. Her ankle throbbed and the choking band around her throat sent waves of panic through her.

"Mr. Blake, please forgive me for being so ungrateful. I should not have run off on you . . ." It crushed her to utter the words, but it seemed like the only way to change her circumstances. "Please punish me as you see fit."

"Do you *want* me to punish you?"

She responded only by meeting his glare with a hateful one of her own.

"I said, do you want me to punish you? Answer now or I'll leave you here for the next twenty-four hours."

At least if he bent her over a punishment bench, she wasn't in danger of choking to death.

"Yes," she ground out. "Please punish me, Mr. Blake."

He stood up and walked behind her. She could hear his footsteps as he walked across the room, then returned.

"Although you are an unworthy slut, I am willing to rehabilitate you."

She felt the bars move away from her ass as he opened a door positioned—she was sure not accidentally—right over her behind.

She jumped as his fingers stroked over her round flesh, then his hand connected with her ass in a sharp slap, the sound filling the room.

"Do you like that?"

"Yes, Mr. Blake," she lied. To do otherwise would trigger his wrath.

"Good. If you like that, then you'll love the riding crop."

Then he stepped back and she felt a sharp stinging across her ass. She yelped at the pain. Then he slashed it against her again. She arched forward, regretting it instantly as the collar tightened. He wrapped an arm around her waist and pulled her back hard against the cage, then he whacked her again. And again.

She sucked in air, trying to ignore the burning pain.

"Your ass looks quite appealing bright red like that." He stroked one cheek, then smacked it with his hand.

She had to force herself not to pull away from his repulsive touch.

She was rewarded when he released the fastener holding her wrist attached to the bars. Then the other one. She lifted her arms, which were stiff and numb. She squeezed and flexed her fingers, and moved her arms to get the circulation moving.

But instead of untying the cords holding her neck and feet immobile, Donovan sat down in the chair in front of her.

"Touch yourself."

"What?"

His passive expression tightened in annoyance. "I said touch yourself."

She glared at him. "Fuck you!"

Fury flashed in his eyes and she instantly regretted her rebelliousness. He stood up. Her chest constricted as he strode toward her. What would he do to her?

But as he got closer, he schooled his features and appeared very calm.

He walked behind the cage and wrapped his hand around her throat, his fingers gliding back and forth along the edge of the collar.

"I'm going to fuck you," he murmured near her ear. "So hard you won't be able to stand for a week." His fingers tightened on her neck. "Then I'm going to do it again. And again."

Blind panic gripped her and she sucked in a breath.

Suddenly, the front door burst open.

"Get away from her right now or you're a dead man."

Steele!

She couldn't see him, since the door was behind her, but relief surged through her, knowing he was here to save her.

Donovan tightened his hold around her neck, and she feared he was going to thrust into her despite Steele's presence, but then someone pulled him back.

In her relief, her muscles sagged and the collar tightened painfully as her body sank. Panic rushed through her, but it was as if her body had given up now that help was here.

Wild Card dodged in front of her. "Fuck, she's choking. Someone get over here and help me."

There were shouts and the sound of a struggle behind her.

Big hands wrapped around her hips through the bars behind her and lifted her slouching body, loosening the collar a little, as Wild Card fumbled with the door in front. She sucked in a breath.

"Hold her while I get this collar undone," Shock said behind her.

Wild Card wrapped his arm around her waist and held her tight to him and lifted her, taking her weight. The pressure on her throat loosened and she fell forward against Wild Card's solid shoulder.

"Wait, now I need to get these shoes off her. Fuck, give me your knife."

Wild Card continued to hold her as he reached in his pocket, then handed the pocket knife to Shock. She tensed as she felt the back of the blade glide along her ankle, under the strap of the shoe, but he jerked it away from her, cutting the leather and not her. A second later, he freed her from the other strap, too.

"One of her ankles is swollen badly. Be careful."

Wild Card helped her step forward out of the shoes, supporting her body. He drew her from the cage with infinite care, then lifted her in his arms and carried her to the armchair. He gently set her down, then pulled off his leather jacket and covered her with it.

She clutched the soft leather and pulled it around her. She saw the others now. Dom and Magic gripped Donovan's arms tightly. Steele strode to her and sank to his knees in front of her. His fingers stroked lightly against her cheek.

"Are you all right, baby?" he asked in a hoarse whisper.

She nodded, tears prickling at her eyes. "Now that you're here."

Shock handed Steele a blanket and he tucked it around her gently. She clung to it, just wanting to get out of here, but at the same time needing to get her bearings.

He slid his hands behind her neck and carefully unbuckled the thick collar. As soon as it loosened, she sucked in a big gulp of air. He ran his fingers gently over her tender throat.

"What did that bastard do to you?" he muttered under his breath. Then he turned and glared at Donovan.

In a flash, he lurched to his feet and stormed toward Donovan. His fist connected with the man's jaw. Dom and Magic let him go and stepped out of Steele's way. In shock, she watched as Steele pulled the man to his feet and hit him again then, when he was down, Steele kept on pounding his fist into Donovan's face.

"No, Steele. Please stop," she cried. "You'll kill him."

"He deserves it for what he did to you," Wild Card said.

She glanced to Shock. "Please don't let him do this," she begged.

Shock nodded and stood up.

"Steele," he said as he strode toward him. "That's enough."

He nodded his head to Dom and Magic. They grabbed Steele and pulled him off the bleeding man. He struggled against them. "Fuck, let me go."

"Steele. He's not worth it," Laurie implored.

He glared at the man on the ground, his fists clenched at his sides. "But you are," he answered with gritted teeth.

"Please, Steele. For me. Just let it go."

Steele's heart pounded as he stared at the man lying on the floor. He wanted to pummel the life out of the asshole. He wanted to wrap his hands around his throat and squeeze out his last breath.

When he'd seen him standing behind Laurie, all his fears brought to life as he saw the man about to rape her, a murderous rage had built inside him. He'd held it at bay still hoping that Laurie was all right, then when he saw the truth, it had consumed him.

If Laurie hadn't stopped him, he would have kept on hitting the man until he was a bloody, lifeless husk. But Laurie wanted him to stop and the saner part of him knew that if he killed the man, he'd wind up in prison, no matter what the other man's crimes had been. And if he was in prison, he couldn't be with Laurie. And that was all that mattered to him now.

He took a step back, then turned and walked toward her. He knelt in front of her again, his gaze falling to the redness on her throat where her weight had pressed against the too-tight collar when her body had sagged. The sadistic son of a bitch had probably kept her in that cage all night.

He stroked her hair from her face. "It's all right now."

He glanced over his shoulder to Dom. "Put the collar on the asshole and put him in the cage."

He turned back to face her and stroked her cheek. "Sweetheart, let me get those straps off your wrists."

She brought one hand out from under the blanket and he unfastened the strap. As his fingers worked on the buckle, he caught a glimpse of blood on her skin, below the shoulder, and his gut clenched. She offered the other wrist and once he had them both off, he tossed them to Magic.

He stroked his finger over the small cut. "What happened here?"

She just shook her head, clearly not ready to talk about it yet.

Wild Card set her jeans on the arm of the chair. "These aren't usable anymore," he said as he held up her bra and panties.

Steele's stomach tightened as he saw they'd been sliced by a knife. That probably explained the cut. And as evil as this bastard was, there were probably more. Wild Card tossed them on the table beside the chair, then he handed Steele a shredded T-shirt.

"I suppose she could wear this backward and tie it somehow," Wild Card suggested.

"No need." Raven walked toward them and pulled off

her jacket. She tugged her shirt over her head, revealing a black push-up bra beneath. She tossed the shirt to Steele, then pulled on her jacket and zipped it up.

"She doesn't look in very good shape to be riding on the back of a bike," Raven pointed out.

"We have no choice," Steele answered.

"I'll be okay," Laurie said as she pulled Wild Card's jacket from under the blanket and handed it to him.

She took Raven's shirt and pulled it on, then she slid on the jeans under the blanket, feeling painfully vulnerable after the attack. She pushed aside the blanket, then tried to stand up, but immediately winced and dropped back in the chair. Steele saw her swollen ankle.

"You're not walking anywhere on that."

Magic handed Steele the comfortable, black, tie-up shoes Laurie had been traveling in. He slipped each one on her, being careful of her sore ankle, and tied them loosely, then he lifted her from the chair.

"What about him?" Rip asked, nudging his head to Donovan, who was now in the cage, his neck and wrists fastened to the bars.

"Don't worry. We'll alert the police to his situation. In a few hours."

"You're going to regret this," Donovan shouted from the cage. "That slut is going to bring you more trouble than you ever bargained for."

Steele carried her outside and the door slammed on Donovan's empty threats. Steele set her on the front of his bike, then fastened a helmet beneath her chin. He stroked her cheek. "I'm never going to let you out of my sight again. I promise you that."

He smiled and kissed her gently, then he mounted behind her and started up his bike, relief surging through him that she was finally in his protective keep again.

Steele and the others hadn't ridden very far before he felt Laurie drooping. If the asshole had kept her in that cage all night, she wouldn't have gotten any real sleep. She had to be exhausted.

A road sign indicated a town about ten miles ahead. As they got closer, he saw a motel along the side of the road. He signaled for the others to pull over and they all turned into the parking lot.

He pulled off his helmet as the others parked in a row beside him.

"It's been a long night. We're all pretty tired. Let's get some rooms and relax."

"I'm all for that," Shock said. "I'll go in and get us set up."

Laurie still leaned back against him. He handed his helmet to Wild Card, then unfastened her helmet and pulled it off. Wild Card stowed both away.

Steele stroked her hair from her face. "You doing okay?"

She tipped her head back and gazed up at him. "I am now that I'm with you."

At her words, and the soft glow in her eyes, warmth

filled him. He loved this woman. He would do anything to protect her. And to make her happy.

Shock returned and handed Steele a key, then tossed keys to the others. Steele dismounted and scooped Laurie up, then carried her to room nineteen and opened the door. Carrying her over the threshold like this made him think of white lace and promises of a lifetime together.

That was something he'd never thought he wanted before, but now he craved it . . . with her.

He pushed the door closed behind him and carried her to the bed, then set her down. He turned around to see the curtains fully open and the crew smiling in at him. He strode to the window, a grin on his face, and pulled the curtains closed, blocking out their friendly faces.

This would actually be his first time alone with Laurie in a bed, since they'd become intimate, and he would take every advantage of it. Not that he expected anything from her. He just wanted to hold her close. Feel her body against his, and know she was safe in his arms.

He just wanted to cherish her.

He pulled back the covers. He knelt in front of her and untied her shoes, then pulled them off. He suppressed the urges that threatened to rise in him. She'd been through a horrible ordeal. He was not going to do anything to make her uncomfortable.

"I'll go grab my stuff from the bike and get you a nice, clean shirt to sleep in."

She nodded as he slipped outside. When he returned, she was in bed, the covers pulled up to her neck. He riffled through his bag and grabbed a T-shirt. He placed it on the bed beside her, then turned back to grab a change of clothes from his bag, giving her privacy.

When he turned back, she was gazing at him.

The room had two double beds and as much as he wanted to climb into bed with her, to hold her tight in his arms, he realized he needed to give her time after her ordeal. He kicked off his shoes, then sat down on the other bed, but she pushed back the covers on her bed.

"Don't you want to be with me?" she asked, looking uncertain and a little vulnerable.

"Of course, I just . . . I mean, after what you've been through I just thought you might need space."

"What I need is you. I want to feel you close. I want you to hold me."

He shifted to her bed and slid in beside her, then wrapped his arms around her and drew her close. He kissed her temple. "It's okay, baby. I'm never going to leave you alone again."

Soon she was asleep in his arms. He reveled in the feel of her so close to him, her soft hair pressed against his cheek. Finally, his own exhaustion overtook him.

Laurie's eyelids popped open and she glanced around. Where was she? The last she remembered she was . . . oh, God, Donovan had grabbed her and stuck her in that cage. But then Steele showed up and saved her.

Panic welled up. Where was he now?

"Steele?" She bolted to a sitting position.

"What is it, sweetheart?" Steele glanced up from a magazine he was reading. He sat in an armchair in the motel room he'd brought her to. He put the magazine down and walked toward her, his features etched with concern. "Nightmare?"

"I just . . . I wasn't sure where you were."

He sat down on the bed beside her and stroked back her hair with a sweet tenderness that touched her heart. "I told you, I'll never leave you alone again."

His words, and his gentle touch, made her want him with a desperation that dug deep into her soul. She grasped his hand and kissed his palm, wanting to let the covers fall from her body and expose her naked breasts to him. Wanting to draw his hand to her breast and press it over her. But something stopped her.

Then he frowned and his fingers stroked over her skin, just below her shoulder. "That son of a bitch cut you."

She glanced down and saw his fingertip stroke over the small cut where Donovan had nicked her with his knife when he'd cut away her bra strap. Steele's gaze took in the cuts on both sides. The dried blood caked over them made them seem worse than they really were.

The concern in his eyes tore at her heart and she was glad he couldn't see the others right now.

"Thank you for coming for me." She didn't want to imagine what would have happened if Steele hadn't burst in when he had. She wanted to thank him more sincerely. Wanted to somehow make him understand how much it meant to her.

He stroked her cheek, his granite eyes warm and caring. "I wish I'd gotten there sooner."

He leaned toward her and brushed his lips to hers. His arms swept around her and she lost herself in his kiss, her heart aching with a need to be closer.

"Steele, I want . . ." She gazed into his eyes, but she didn't know what to say. She wanted to be close to him. To be intimate. But the thought sent her stomach churning.

"What is it?" He gazed at her with such concern.

"I want to be close to you. To . . ." She blinked back tears, fighting the fear inside her.

"Sweetheart, after what you've been through, you need time." He cupped her face in his hands. "We don't have to rush anything."

She nodded. Thankful for his understanding, yet still yearning for that closeness.

He drew her into his arms and held her close. "Let's just get some more sleep."

He lay down, keeping her snug against his warm, solid body. Holding her. Protecting her. And soon she felt herself drifting off to sleep again.

Steele dragged himself from Laurie's warm, soft body and pushed himself from the bed. He didn't want to leave her side, but he knew she'd be hungry and he wanted to go out and get something for her to eat. After that, they'd be on their way. He knew she'd be anxious to get home. And her brother would be anxious to see her and know firsthand that she was okay.

He went outside, the late afternoon sun casting long shadows on the ground. He mounted his bike and headed to the small town only a few miles farther along the highway.

He went to a drugstore and bought a bandage for Laurie's ankle, then he pulled into a small diner and ordered some burgers to take out. As the cook flipped the patties on the grill, Steele paid.

"I take it you're traveling with friends," the man behind the counter asked.

Steele eyed the man. He wore a blue-and-white bandana around his head and his long, gray hair was tied back in a ponytail. And his arms were inked.

"Why you asking?"

"Just a friendly heads-up. Some cops come in here asking if we seen a crew of bikers in the area. Said there been some kinda trouble up at some bigwig's country house nearby."

The cook handed the bag of burgers to Steele.

"Just figured I'd let you know."

Steele nodded. "Thanks."

Steele went outside and stowed the burgers in his hard carrier, then mounted the bike. The cops must have found Donovan and now he'd set them on their trail.

No matter. This was a complication he did not want, but he'd handle it. First things first. Go back and warn the crew.

He started up the bike, then sped back to the motel.

When he arrived, Magic, Dom, Wild Card, and Shock

were sitting on chairs outside the rooms drinking beer. Rip
and Raven were nowhere to be seen.

He saw the curtain pull back on his room and Laurie
peer out. As he stopped his bike, she hurried out of the
room. She was still limping and he wanted to get her to a
doctor to have her ankle checked out.

"Where's Rip?" Steele asked.

Shock pointed at Rip's room door. Steele walked over
and knocked. A moment later, Rip opened the door and
peered out.

"We have trouble," Steele said. "The police have been
asking around town about us. They're sure to be checking the motels nearby."

Rip grabbed his cell as he stepped outside, then dialed.

"Killer, it's Rip." Rip paced back and forth as he listened.

"Is everything okay?" Laurie asked, concern in her
eyes. "Do you think they found Donovan and he's convinced them to come after us?"

Steele placed his hands on her shoulders and locked
gazes with her. "He hurt you, remember? You have nothing to be afraid of."

She shook her head. "No. If he wants to make trouble,
he'll do it. If he wants to get back at me . . . or you . . .
he'll do it. He'll buy people off if he has to."

Steele glanced toward Rip, who had paced several yards
away and was speaking intently on the phone.

"He won't buy off Killer. He's a true friend."

Rip slipped his phone into his pocket and walked

toward Steele, his expression grim. Laurie reached for Steele's hand and he enveloped it in his.

"Well?" Steel prompted.

Rip glanced at Laurie, then back to Steele. "They found Donovan a few hours ago at his house. He was dead."

Laurie sucked in a breath and Steele squeezed her hand.

Rip gazed at Laurie again. "And the police are looking for you." His lips compressed in a tight line. "You're wanted for questioning."

Aftershock

Laurie felt faint. She clung to Steele's hands as the blood rushed from her face.

"I can't believe this. Are they sure? How could he be dead?" she asked.

"Killer said to hang tight and he'll fill us in on the details when he gets back to us." Rip grasped her shoulder and squeezed. "But, I'm sorry, Donovan is definitely dead."

"So this means the police are coming here for me?" she said weakly, her hand trembling.

"You're white as a ghost," Steele said, gazing at her. "Let's get you inside."

He led her into their room and the others followed. She sat on the bed and Steele sat beside her while the others gathered around, looking somber.

"Laurie, you didn't do anything wrong," Rip said. "It's going to be all right."

She glanced at Steele, remembering his fist hammering into Donovan's face. Oh, God, was that why he'd died?

Because Steele had beat him and then they'd left him in that cage? Had he died from injuries inflicted by Steele? If they had called someone sooner, would Donovan still be alive?

The thought sent a shock wave through her.

She'd hated Donovan. She hated what he'd done to her. She hated how cruel he'd been. And he'd terrified her. Just knowing he was out there had kept her in fear.

But knowing he was dead, and that Steele might have something to do with it, left her feeling numb.

"I don't know what to tell them. I don't know . . ." She was shaking her head and realized it was all too much. She felt weak and scared and . . . traumatized.

Rip sat on the other side of her.

"You'll just tell them the truth. That the guy kidnapped you . . . terrorized you . . . then we showed up and pulled you out of there."

"But won't they charge you with breaking and entering? What about the fact that . . ." She gazed at Steele, then back to Rip, and continued hesitantly. "Donovan was beaten up. What if that's why he died? What if they charge . . ." She shot a quick glance to Steele again, then bit her lip.

Steele's granite eyes glinted. "You think I'm responsible for his death?" Steele murmured in a mere whisper.

His face clouded and she realized as much as he hated Donovan, he didn't want to be responsible for his death.

She squeezed his hand. "You were saving me. You were reacting to what he did to me. You didn't mean to . . ."

"Let's just all keep calm," Shock said. "Rip said Killer

is going to call us back. Let's not get worked up about what might happen. We'll face whatever we have to when the time comes."

"That's good advice," Rip agreed. "Steele, you went out to get food, right?"

Steele nodded.

"Okay, let's all just eat and relax. Killer should get back to us soon." Rip stood up and headed for the door.

Dom went with him and they returned a few minutes later with a brown paper bag and the case of beer the guys had been sharing outside. Dom opened a bottle and handed it to Laurie. She took a sip, then just stared at the burger Rip placed in her hand. Her stomach growled at the smell of food, so she unwrapped the paper around it, but after one bite, put it down beside her.

Silence hung in the air as everyone ate. Steele encouraged her to eat a little more and she finished about half, then gave up. It tasted like sawdust in her mouth.

"Hey, this place has a pool," Raven said. "Why don't we be real badasses and go swimming even though we've just eaten?" She grinned.

It was a warm day, and the thought of relaxing in the sparkling water had its appeal, but Laurie shook her head.

"You all go ahead. I'll stay here."

Raven looked hesitant, then put her hand on Laurie's. "I'm just trying to get your mind off all this, since there's nothing we can do right now."

Laurie took a deep breath. "Thanks, Raven, but I'm just not up to it."

"It's okay. I'll stay with her," Steele said. "Rip, just leave the phone with me in case Killer calls."

"You got it." Rip stood up and pulled the cell from his pocket and handed it to Steele. "The pool's just around the corner of the building, so if you need us, let us know."

Steele nodded and they all filed out and Dom, the last one out, closed the door behind them.

Laurie turned to Steele and rested her hand on his cheek. "Oh, Steele, I'm so sorry I got you into this mess."

"It wasn't your fault. You were a victim in all this."

She shook her head. "No. I chose to go out with him. I made the mistake of not seeing Donovan for what he really was. You tried to protect me and now you and your crew are pulled into this whole thing."

"Don't worry about us. You've been through a terrible ordeal. It's you I'm concerned about." He wrapped his arms around her and pulled her close. "I'd do anything to protect you. Anything."

She rested her head against his chest, listening to his heartbeat. Letting the steady rhythm and the feel of his strong arms holding her tight calm her. She could drift into sleep right here in his arms. Just let her cares slip away and surrender to unconsciousness.

He stroked her hair and she tightened her arms around his waist. They sat there quietly, just holding each other. In the distance she could hear the others splashing in the pool. She closed her eyes and just let her thoughts go, surrendering to nothingness.

The cell phone rang, and she jumped.

Steele pulled the phone from his pocket.

"Steele here." He gazed at her grimly. "Yeah, we've been waiting for your call."

She heard the rhythm of the voice on the line, but not the words.

Steele answered questions, explaining what had happened. He glanced at her a few times.

"Yeah, she's pretty shaken up, but physically okay. Except for a few cuts and a twisted ankle."

She shifted beside him.

"No, we haven't taken her to a doctor. It doesn't seem to be broken, but it is swollen."

Steele gave a few more details about the attack, telling him about the cage and admitting that he had hit Donovan.

"He was in the cage when we left him."

Her stomach clenched.

After a few more minutes, he hung up.

"He said we should just stay put and hold off on going to a doctor for your ankle right now, unless it's really bad. He wants to save you the stress of being picked up until he knows more."

"My ankle's fine," she said. It hurt when she walked and the swelling made it uncomfortable, but she could live with that.

Steele insisted she lay back and put it up, then he fetched ice in a plastic bag, wrapped it in a towel, and arranged it on her ankle. When the others returned about a half hour later, Steele wrapped her ankle in a bandage he'd bought when he'd gone to get the burgers earlier and they filled up the time playing cards and drinking.

After ordering a late dinner of pizza, they all returned to their rooms to get some sleep.

Laurie felt the blackness closing in on her, stifling her breathing. A hand clutched her throat, choking her. She tried to flee, but she couldn't move. Her hands were restrained. She murmured, unable to scream, fear exploding through her.

She tried to kick, but her legs wouldn't move. Panic blazed through her.

"Laurie."

Her eyelids popped open. Darkness surrounded her. A body was pressed against her. Big and hard. A man's strong arms were wrapped around her.

Oh, God, Donovan. Memories of the cage he'd locked her in flashed through her brain. Fear and anguish gripped her.

She lurched forward, scrambling from his hold, and scurried through the darkness. She didn't know where she was. But her ankle buckled and she fell to the floor.

The light snapped on and she rolled onto her butt, then pushed herself backward with her one good foot and her hands, but found herself trapped in a corner of the room.

"Laurie, what the hell?" Steele was still half asleep, but at the sight of Laurie on the ground panting, he became fully alert. He pushed himself from the bed and walked toward her slowly.

She cowered in the corner, like a trapped animal, her eyes glazed in fear.

He crouched on the floor, still several feet away. "It's okay, baby. Did you have a nightmare?"

Her gaze darted back and forth as she sucked in deep breaths. Did she even recognize him?

"Laurie. It's okay. You're safe now. You're here with me."

She focused on him, her eyes wide, and seemed to relax a little.

"Steele?" she said hesitantly.

"That's right, Laurie."

Then tears welled in her eyes and flowed down her cheeks. His heart clenched at the sight.

"I . . . I . . ." She sucked in a breath.

He sat down on the floor. "It's okay. Just take it slowly."

"I was in a cage. He tried to choke me. I was so scared."

The words tumbled from her mouth in a rapid flow, punctuated by shallow breaths.

"I know, baby."

He wanted to pull her into his arms and comfort her, but he didn't want to approach her. All he could do was be here for her and wait for her to come to him.

She sucked in a few more breaths, then her gaze turned to his. "It was real, wasn't it? It wasn't just a nightmare."

He nodded.

She started to tremble. She pulled her knees close and wrapped her arms around herself.

He moved closer. She stiffened a little, so he stopped.

"It's all right now. You're safe," he crooned.

She stared at him, wide, glistening eyes, almost hopeful.

He opened his arms. She hesitated for a moment, but then she pushed forward the short distance between them. He took her in his arms and pulled her onto his lap, holding her close. She rested her head against his chest and he stroked her hair. He could feel the dampness on his shirt as her tears flowed.

"You saved me," she murmured. "Thank you for finding me."

"Of course. I told you, I'd do anything to protect you."

They sat like that for a while, him holding her in the comfort of his arms, then he lifted her and carried her back to the bed. She snuggled into his arms under the covers and he stroked her back, until her breathing became soft and regular. She was asleep.

He laid there, his anger at what had happened to her smoldering within him. He would do his best to protect her forever, but even after death, Donovan's actions preyed on her.

How could he protect her from her nightmares?

A knock sounded on the door. Laurie opened her eyes and sunlight danced across her face. She was in Steele's strong, comforting arms. She closed her eyes again.

The nightmare last night had shaken her, but Steele had been there to calm her and take care of her. His arms tightened around her now.

Another knock.

"Yeah?" Steele called, his voice hoarse from sleep.

Laurie shifted in his arms, but kept her eyes closed, not ready to be jarred from this comforting cocoon just yet.

"It's Rip. Can I come in?"

"Yeah, hold on."

She opened her eyes and met Steele's dark eyes.

"Do you think he's heard from Killer?" she asked.

His lips brushed the crown of her head in a tender kiss. "Let's go find out."

He pushed himself from the bed and walked to the door. Laurie pulled the covers close to her as he opened the door. Rip stood on the other side and Steele stepped back to let him come in. He carried two Starbucks cups in his hand.

Rip glanced at Laurie, concern etched in his face. "How are you doing?"

"Okay." Despite her response, she felt small and vulnerable. She wiped sleep from her eyes and wondered if she looked like a lost child, tucked under the bedclothes, clinging to the scant protection of the covers.

Steele took the coffees from Rip and handed one to Laurie. She took a thankful sip of the steaming liquid.

"Killer just called," Rip said.

Laurie's heart rate accelerated, her focus locking on him. She watched as Rip walked to the second bed and sat down, facing her.

"We'll have to go in for questioning."

Her heart clenched. She had hoped this would all just go away.

"But it's okay," he continued.

Steele sat beside Laurie and slid his arm around her. "What do you mean, it's okay?"

"They know it wasn't us."

"How?" she asked, hope coiling through her.

"When they found him, he wasn't in the cage." Rip stretched his long legs out in front of him. "There were two guys who worked for him. They showed up a few hours after we left and found him. When they let him out, apparently he became belligerent and started a fight with them. He fell and hit his head on the corner of the glass coffee table and cracked his skull."

"And these guys admitted all that?"

"Not at first. Especially since they panicked and fled the scene, but there's evidence proving he died from hitting his head and where. Once they were picked up they just filled in the details. Now we have to go in to give our statements."

"Are you going to be in trouble for breaking in when you all came to save me?" she asked.

Rip gazed at her. "They know what he did to you. Donovan's men admitted to kidnapping you and helping him lock you in the cage, then leaving you there. Killer told me they're not charging us with a thing."

Laurie drew her arms from around Steele's waist. As he dismounted the bike, she stared at her town house.

The bright purple-and-pink petunias she had planted several weeks ago had filled out nicely and the golden-yellow Stella D'Oro lilies were cheerfully blooming. The wreath she'd crafted from lavender and pink calico fabric, silk flowers, and lacy ribbons adorned the lemon-yellow door, and the mat, with WELCOME written in a lovely script, surrounded by curlicues and flowers in pink-and-green pastel, was warm and inviting.

And familiar.

That should give her comfort. She should feel happy returning home, but instead she felt a lead weight in her stomach.

It had been so long since she'd been here and her whole life had changed in the time away.

"You look so serious," Steele said, watching her. "Aren't you happy to be home?"

She smiled. "Sure. I'm just taking it all in."

Steele helped her from the bike. Even though her ankle was feeling much better now, she'd gotten used to Steele babying her, and it felt good being taken care of by him.

Being loved by him.

He hadn't said the words, but she could see it in his eyes. And she felt the same way.

Just like returning home, that should make her happy, but it just left her feeling unsettled.

She handed Steele her helmet and smiled. "You don't mind staying here without your men?"

"It'd be pretty crowded in your small place with all seven of us. I'm sure the others are quite happy back at the cabin." His arms came around her and he drew her close, then kissed her soundly. "And I'm looking forward to some private time with you."

Most of the days they'd spent on the road getting home they'd camped under the stars as they typically did, which allowed no privacy.

His words and the heat in his eyes reminded her they hadn't made love since before . . .

Her gut clenched. She didn't want to think about Donovan. She wanted to put that whole part of her life behind her.

Steele grabbed his pack and took her hand as they walked to the entrance. Three young women walked along the sidewalk, glancing her way as she walked toward the front door with the big, tattooed Steele beside her, and she smiled at the obvious envy in their eyes.

She unlocked the front door and Steele followed her into the entryway. As soon as the door closed, he pulled her into his arms again and kissed her, his tongue gliding between her lips, then caressing the inside of her mouth. When he finally released her, she was breathless with need.

He seemed to fill the place with his big, broad-shouldered frame. He glanced around, taking in her feminine paraphernalia. "Nice place."

She glanced up at him with a smile. "You don't find it too girly?"

He drew her close, holding her tight to his hard, masculine planes. "I find it sweet and pretty, just like you."

His hands glided down her sides, and over her hips, then his mouth swooped down and captured hers. She melted against him, feeling soft and feminine against his hardness.

Then she felt another hardness, pressing against her belly. His arms suddenly felt like ropes coiled around her, his body big and menacing. She stiffened, her heart suddenly racing.

This isn't Donovan. I'm not trapped.

She tried to calm her erratic breathing, but she needed space. She pressed him back and he easily yielded, releasing her.

She pasted a smile on her face and gazed up at him. "I just want to get in and settled. I think I'll go shower and change. Why don't you grab a cold drink from the kitchen, then I'll take you on a tour?"

She escaped to the bathroom, then closed the door and leaned against it. What had come over her? Steele had been protective and caring of her ever since he'd met her. He was not Donovan.

She stripped off the biker chick clothing she'd borrowed from Raven and stepped into the shower stall. As the water ran over her, she heard the bathroom door open.

"I could use a shower, too," Steele said from outside the foggy glass door.

She heard his jeans hit the floor, then his other clothes follow. She turned as he opened the glass door.

"Room for one more?"

The sight of him . . . big, tattooed, and muscular . . . took her breath away. All she could do was nod. He dwarfed any space, so it would be a tight squeeze with both of them in such a small shower stall, but she wanted him here. She wanted to feel his body close to hers. To feel him stroke and hold her.

He closed the glass door behind him and picked up the soap, his dark gaze gliding over her naked body. He lathered up his hands, then stroked them over her shoulders, then down to her breasts. His big hands covered her, and her nipples puckered to hard nubs. She turned her back to him and he cupped her breasts, caressing them, then drew her back against his body.

The water careened down on them and her heart beat rapidly as he stroked her breasts, then glided his hands along her hips. She wanted to grind her behind back against his growing erection, to open her legs and lean forward in open invitation. She wanted him to make love to her. Now. Here.

She ached for him.

Steele drew her back against him, his lips nuzzling her neck, his arm coming around her waist. Drawing her back against his hard body.

But the space was small and memories of being locked in the small cage Donovan had trapped her in flashed through her. Memories of Donovan's arm around her waist, pulling her tight against the cage. Her stomach clenched.

I'm going to fuck you. So hard you won't be able to stand for a week. Then I'm going to do it again. And again.

Donovan's words ripped through her brain and she froze. Panic welled in her.

She shoved away Steele's arm and pushed past him,

scurrying from the shower. She grabbed a towel as she hurried out the door and into her bedroom, closing the door behind her.

Steele's gut clenched as the door closed behind Laurie.

Fuck, he was pushing too much. But he had been careful with her for days, treating her like a fragile doll. Loving, sensitive, and understanding.

He had only been trying to ease them gently into what he knew they both wanted. And needed.

When she looked at him, he could see the hunger in her eyes. She wanted physical intimacy just as much as he did. Maybe even more. But she was frightened. And traumatized by that bastard.

He wanted to help her, but he didn't know what to do.

He washed his hair and scrubbed his body, then stepped out of the shower and dried off. With a towel casually draped around his waist, he went into the living room and pulled out some clean clothes from his bag and donned them.

He could definitely use some coffee. He walked into her kitchen and found coffee and filters in the cupboard then put on a pot. As he waited for the pot to fill, he leaned against the counter and glanced around. A flowery picture was on the wall and a silk flower arrangement on the small rectangular table in the corner. A shelf about a foot down from the ceiling held delicate teacups on saucers, and a bookshelf of cookbooks was adorned with little plaques with homey-type sayings.

This was definitely a woman's home. Very feminine, and it gave him a very different view of Laurie than the striking woman in the stilettos and short club-style dress—that her asshole ex had picked out for her—and then the jeans and biker-girl T-shirts, which she'd borrowed from Raven.

He lifted the edge of a frilly, lace-edged pot holder that hung from a hook on the wall and it struck him. He really didn't know anything about Laurie. When she'd been riding with them, she'd been outside her element. Fleeing from an abusive ex, and the law. Living on the edge and just coping the best she could.

This—he took the pot holder in his hand, staring at the words HOME SWEET HOME embroidered in a delicate script—was who she was. She wasn't a woman like Raven who would be willing to give up her life and ride around with a band of bikers, living from day to day. Laurie wanted stability. She wanted a home.

She wanted to be safe.

His heart compressed.

She couldn't find that with him. He was a nomad. Always moving. Never wanting to stay in one place. When he was younger, he'd stayed in Chicago to look out for his sister, to give her a sense of home, but once Chrissy was gone . . .

He shook his head. He wouldn't have changed those years trying to help her, but they'd done no good. And Laurie was a totally different situation. He was sure she'd learned from her mistakes and wouldn't get into a relationship with a man like Donovan again. A man who would abuse her.

Fuck, a man who would dominate her.

What the hell had he been thinking? She didn't want a man in her life who would try to control her. She found it exciting, sure, but who was he kidding?

She couldn't be in a relationship with a dominant man. Not now. Not after what that bastard had done to her.

He opened the door to the cupboard and stared at the cups. They were all pretty, adorned with flowers, butterflies, kittens. He grabbed one with a fluffy kitten staring out a window and another one staring in. It was adorable.

It was totally Laurie.

He poured a cup of coffee and walked into the living room and sat down.

Laurie drew in a deep breath and opened the door to her bedroom. She had to face Steele, and explain what had happened.

She walked into the living room, dressed in her own jeans for the first time in over a week, and a floral halter top. Steele sat on the couch, looking totally incongruous sitting in her distinctly feminine living room, holding her favorite cat mug.

He was too big for this room. Too masculine. To rough and ready.

"You want to talk about it?" he asked.

There was no point asking what. They both knew.

She nodded as she sank into the chair in front of him.

"I'm sorry. I just . . . I keep reliving what happened with Donovan."

He put down his cup and leaned forward, his hands clasped between his knees. "I'm not Donovan. I'm not going to hurt you like he did."

She nodded. "I know."

He raised an eyebrow. "Do you?"

Guilt washed through her. She did know, but she'd been treating him as if she didn't. She stood up and walked toward him, then perched beside him on the couch.

"I'm sorry, Steele." She took his hand and locked gazes with him. "It's not you. You know that. I just have to . . . get past this." She drew his hand to her lips and kissed his rough knuckles. "I know you can help me do that." She leaned forward and kissed the tip of his raspy chin. "Will you help me?"

Steele watched as she reached behind her neck and untied the halter, then lowered it, revealing her naked breasts. His heart clenched and his cock stirred. For days he'd held back, wanting her, but knowing he had to give her time. And every time she pulled back from him, he had died a little inside. He knew she didn't mean to reject him, but that didn't change how it made him feel.

She took his hand again and pressed it to one mound. He groaned softly.

Fuck, he wanted her so bad.

He felt a tug on his jeans as she pulled down his zipper, then her hand slid inside. His heart raced as her delicate fingers wrapped around him.

God, he needed to be inside her. His body ached with the overwhelming need.

He had to fight the compelling drive to shove her back on the couch, tear her clothes away, then drive into her. Hard and fast.

He kept tight control on himself, but what if he got carried away? What if he acted on that need? Would she ever trust him again?

Her fingers glided over his length and he moaned, his hand tightening on her soft breast.

He should stop her.

But he couldn't. Her tender touch met a need deep inside him. Made him feel special and loved. She was like a drug he couldn't shake.

She stroked his cock until it was so stiff he couldn't think straight. Then she stood up and pushed off her jeans, then climbed onto his lap. Her fingers wrapped around him again and she pressed his tip to her hot, melting core.

He grasped her waist. "Oh, God, Laurie, you feel so good."

She stroked his hair back, then smiled as she lowered herself onto him. He almost gasped at the feel of her warmth surrounding him. Being buried inside her was the most exquisite feeling he'd ever experienced.

She lifted and lowered herself, gliding on him in a sweet, passionate caress. His cock ached at the sublime sensations. He closed his eyes and let himself get lost in her.

He filled her again and again as she made love to him, gliding up and down, her loving hands stroking his chest. He groaned as she squeezed him inside and she moaned softly at her own pleasure.

She sped up and the pleasure heightened. She squeezed again and his groin tightened, then he erupted inside her, the pleasure blossoming to pure joy.

She gasped, rocking her hips on him, then moaned as she found her own release.

He held her close as she rested against his chest, all soft and feminine in his arms.

The experience had been incredible. Loving and soft and exciting. It was exactly what she'd needed, and he was happy about that. She'd been in control and set the pace. She'd kept everything exactly the way she needed it.

And he had no problem giving her control. Sometimes.

But could he hold back all the time? Could he stop himself from doing something that would emotionally throw her right back in that cage Donovan had put her in?

Laurie listened to Steele's heartbeat, enjoying the feel of his arms around her. She'd taken a first step and she knew now that they could move forward. Feeling Steele inside her . . . his big cock filling her as she'd moved on him . . . had been heaven.

And he'd been so patient with her. So loving.

She knew she could trust him to be there for her. To give her what she needed.

She gazed up at him and smiled, but he seemed distracted. Distant.

She stroked his cheek. "Is there something wrong?"

"What, baby?" He met her gaze. "No, of course not." He kissed her, a gentle brush of his lips. "Just tired."

He stroked her hair back, and his gentle touch made her feel warm and protected. "Are you okay? I mean, was that okay?"

She smiled, warmed by his concern. She leaned in and kissed him again. "It was wonderful," she murmured.

He nodded, but she could tell he was unsettled. Well, she had freaked out every time he'd touched her for the past few days. He was definitely still gun-shy.

"How about you just relax while I make some dinner?" She stood up and pulled on her jeans, and she didn't miss the heat of his gaze on her bare breasts as she tucked them back into her halter top and tied it behind her neck.

He stood up. "I think I'll go out for a ride."

She glanced at him in surprise, but didn't say anything.

"Okay. There's a spare key in the bowl by the door." Laurie watched him walk to the door, pick up the key, then close the door behind him.

As hard as these past few days had been on her, they'd been hard on him, too. She thought he'd be happy that they had taken this step forward, but something was bothering him and she wished she knew what it was.

But right now, he needed a little space.

All she knew was, now that she'd allowed herself to open the door and share intimacy with him again, she needed more. He'd stoked the fire and it was blazing inside her.

After dinner, she'd show him just how much she needed him all over again.

Steele mounted his bike and let out the throttle. The roar of the engine was comforting. Reliable. As he rode the bike along the road, the wind whipping at his face, the machine felt like a part of him.

The moment he'd slid from Laurie's body when she'd stood up, he'd ached at the loss of her warmth surrounding him. She'd become a drug he was addicted to. A need that had buried itself deep in the pit of his stomach.

He wanted her. Emotionally. And physically. But he needed more than the sweet, delicate lovemaking they'd just shared.

He knew she needed time. She needed tenderness and love to get past the trauma she'd endured at the hands of Donovan. And he'd give her that. He'd give her whatever she needed.

But what if he fucked up? What if his urges—his intense desire to bend her to his will—got the best of him and he did something stupid? Something that scared her. Or traumatized her even more than what Donovan had done.

Not that he'd do something worse. But coming from him . . . someone she'd learned to trust and rely on . . .

Fuck.

•   •   •

It was close to seven and Laurie stirred the chili again, wondering where Steele was. She walked back to the living room, a glass of red wine in her hand, and sank onto the couch. Steele was used to total freedom. Keeping his own hours. He probably wouldn't appreciate her telling him to be home for dinner at a certain time.

The two of them were so different, lived such different lifestyles, but somehow they would find a way to make things work.

She heard a key in the lock and Steele stepped inside.

He glanced at her, but he seemed preoccupied. "Dinner smells good."

She stood up and walked toward the kitchen. "I hope you like chili. There are homemade buns, too."

He nodded. "That sounds great."

"Okay. Well, sit down and be comfortable, I'll go serve it up."

He sat on the couch. "I could use a beer, too."

"Coming up."

She returned with two bowls of chili and the beer and set one bowl in front of him on the coffee table, then returned for the rolls and butter. They put on an adventure movie while they ate.

She wanted to ask him what was bothering him, but she realized she needed to let him talk in his own time. When they were finished, she cleared away the dishes and sat beside him. She cuddled up to him, and he slid his arm around her, then drew her close. A few minutes later, he tipped up her chin and kissed her, his lips moving softly on hers.

But then he pulled back, staring at her with eyes filled with heated need and anxiety.

"I want to do this with you. I want . . ." He sat back, his hands balled into fists. "But . . . Fuck, I don't want to do anything wrong."

"You won't." She rested her hand on his muscular arm. "I want this, too." She tightened her fingers around him, gazing at him imploringly. "Please, Steele. Make love to me."

A growl rumbled from deep inside him and he pulled her into a deep kiss, then he slid his arm under her knees and he scooped her up and carried her to the bedroom. Silently, he stripped off her clothes, slowly and purposefully, then he stood up and shed his own. Her gaze wandered over his glorious, muscular, tattooed body. Sculpted arms, broad shoulders, ridged abs. Everything about this man was spectacular.

And his cock. It had grown to an impressive length, and it was so thick. He pressed her back on the bed and prowled over her, then kissed her deeply. He tested her readiness by gliding his fingers over her slit, finding slick wetness, then he pressed his cock against her. She drew in a breath as he glided into her, filling her with his thick, hard shaft. She tightened around him, embracing him in the most intimate way she knew how.

He moaned. His lips found hers and he began to move. Drawing out, then gliding deep again. Drawing out, then gliding deep again. He set a smooth, sweet rhythm, driving her pleasure higher and higher with each stroke.

She trembled with need, wanting him with an intensity she'd never known before. She kissed him under the chin, his whiskers raspy against her lips.

Joyous feelings swelled within her. Feelings she couldn't keep to herself.

"Oh, Steele. I love you."

He sped up, driving deep into her. Again and again. She held tight, riding the intense waves of sensation. Then he thrust deep and groaned.

The feel of his liquid heat filling her catapulted her over the edge. She clung to him, as rippling sensations quivered through her, then her body exploded in the sweet ecstasy of release.

Once the shimmering orgasm waned, she collapsed against him and wrapped her arms tightly around his waist. She drifted into sleep, his big cock still inside her.

Laurie awoke with a start. The big warm body she expected to be in her arms was gone.

She pushed back the covers and stood up, then grabbed her robe. Had Steele left?

She walked into the living room and her anxiety waned when she saw him sitting on the couch, a coffee in his hand.

"Good morning."

But he just nodded, then gestured to the couch.

"Laurie, sit down. We need to talk."

Uh-oh.

She settled beside him. "Sounds serious," she said, trying to keep her tone light.

He glanced at her, then stared at his coffee.

"Look, who are we kidding? You and I are never going to work."

Shock vaulted through her and her heart compressed. "I don't understand. Why do you say that?"

He shrugged. "Look around. You have a home here. It reflects who you are and what you want. Stability. Security. You aren't going to get any of that with me."

"Steele, I want to be with you."

Irritation flared in his eyes. "You might think you want me, but I don't believe you'll be happy if you leave your normal life to ride with me, and I can't see myself giving up the open road to live in one place."

She sat there, numb. The thought of leaving her home behind was unsettling, but now that she'd come to terms with her feelings for Steele, she was sure they could work something out. Love could find a way.

She didn't want it to end between them, and she couldn't believe Steele was willing to throw away what they had.

Maybe she should be practical, but her heart didn't care about practicalities. Her heart wanted Steele.

She wanted Steele.

"And even if that weren't true," he continued at her silence, "you need to figure out how to be who you are. You got way in over your head with your relationship with your ex. You figured out it wasn't right and tried to leave, but then you wound up with me. Another Dominant wanting to control you."

She wanted to reach out to him. To stroke her hand over his whisker-roughened cheek. But instead, her hands clenched into fists in her lap.

"But I like being dominated by you," she said. "With you, it's totally different than what he did. You treat me with respect and"—she gazed at him—"love."

His lips compressed. "Look, you were in my care and I protected you. You're right that, fool that I was, I convinced myself I was in love with you. But we were both caught up in high emotional stakes and what I thought was love was just a strong protective instinct."

She shook her head. "I don't believe that. What I saw in your eyes . . . what I feel when you kiss me . . . That's real."

He frowned. "That's passion, not love. You and I have great chemistry together. And what you said last night . . ." His hands clasped between his knees. "You only *think* you love me." He gritted his teeth. "And when you say you like being dominated by me, you don't really get it. You were in my care. You'd been traumatized." He leaned in close, his eyes blazing. "I held back."

"I can handle it."

He stared at her, assessing. "Are you sure about that?"

Her heart pumped faster as he leaned a little closer, his powerful aura filling the room. She wanted him to touch her. To tear the clothes from her. But panic welled in her. And fear. She leaned away a little.

He grabbed her wrists and pushed her down on the couch, trapping her hands beside her head. He captured her mouth, driving his tongue inside. Claiming her.

She could hardly breathe. She was excited, her body trembling with need. Aroused and . . . anxious. Her insides heated as he plundered her mouth, longing for him to take her. He released one of her wrists and slid his hand over her breast, stroking it until her nipple swelled to a tight bud.

"Fuck, I want you." His lips found hers again and he slid his hand under her top, then cupped her breast. His fingers teased her nipple, then he squeezed it between his thumb and finger, leaving her breathless.

His nostrils flared. "Do you still think you can handle it?"

She stared at him wide-eyed, but nodded, then gasped as he grabbed the neckline of her shirt and tore it open, then his mouth found her nipple and he sucked.

He sat up and unzipped his jeans and pulled out his cock. It was hard with wanting her.

He wrapped his fingers around it, the tip jutting from his hand. "Suck me," he ordered.

As soon as she sat up, he pushed her head to his thick cockhead, then filled her mouth with the plum-sized head. He pushed deep, driving into her throat. She gagged but he pulled back, then cupped her head, his fingers forking through her long hair. He glided her head forward and back, his cock sliding in and out of her mouth, more gentle now, but still pushing her to her limit with the thick shaft filling her again and again.

His hand squeezed her head. "Suck me hard."

She gagged again as he drove too deep.

He pulled from her mouth. "I need to be inside you."

He grabbed her jeans and ripped open the tab, then tugged them from her hips, and off. He climbed over her, a look of need on his face.

He tore the crotch of her panties and pressed his cockhead to her damp slit.

She wanted this, oh, so desperately, but a whimper erupted from her throat. It was happening so fast. He was being so demanding.

"No," she cried involuntarily.

He stopped instantly, then drew back. He drew in a breath as he pushed his cock back into his jeans and zipped up.

"That's what I thought."

As she lay there catching her breath, Steele stood up and left the room.

Ten minutes later, he reappeared with his packed bag in his hand.

Her heart clenched at the sight. "You're leaving?"

She wanted desperately for him to deny it. Because she was truly and heart-shatteringly in love with Steele.

"That's right."

"But . . . we just have a few issues to work out," she said desperately. "We just have to—"

"Laurie, no." His granite eyes were steely and distant. "Look, I don't want to hurt you. That's why it's important we recognize this for what it is. If we stay together, either I'll have to hold back, denying who I really am, or I'll wind up hurting you."

She stared at him, still trying to grasp that this was really happening. She didn't believe what he said, but it was clear he had made up his mind and would not be swayed. She drew in a deep breath, then released it. "So this is it?"

His lips compressed. "I'm afraid so. The guys and I will be heading out this afternoon."

Her gaze flicked to his. "So soon?"

"There's no reason to stay any longer."

Ice water trickled through her veins and she trembled. "Of course." Her jaw clenched and she hardened herself against the pain. "Thank you for all you've done for me."

He nodded, then walked to the entrance.

"Take care of yourself," he said with a last glance her way, then disappeared out the door.

As it closed behind him, her heart contracted.

Then the tears flowed.

Steele sped along the highway, his gut aching. He didn't know if he believed what he'd told Laurie or not. His heart insisted he loved her. And maybe she really did love him, too. But he couldn't stay. All the issues he'd brought up *were* true. They were a long way from making a relationship work. And it would kill him to know he'd hurt her.

Better to just let the whole thing go before they got even more involved. So she could find someone who could give her a better life. Someone more stable.

He never wanted to hurt Laurie. If he dominated her in the bedroom, she wouldn't be happy. Especially not after what she'd gone through with Donovan.

He pulled up to the cabin and went inside. The crew was packing up the place.

"Where's Laurie?" Rip asked. "She joining us later?"

"Why did you think I'd be bringing Laurie?"

"Fuck, you kidding man? The two of you are crazy in love. Anyone can see that."

Steele's jaw clenched. "You're wrong." Then he turned and strode off.

A week had passed and Steele couldn't stop thinking about Laurie. He knew he'd done what he had to do, but that didn't make it hurt any less.

They were staying for a couple of weeks at a cottage owned by a friend of Magic's, and Steele had hoped he'd be able to kick back, enjoy the sun and water, and take the time he needed to get over her.

If only it worked that way.

As the sun set, he and the crew rode into town. They were meeting Wild Card at a bar in the small town nearby. They rode along the main street, then pulled up and parked in front of the place, and stepped inside. There was quite a crowd in the place.

"There's Wild Card." Magic grinned. "Hey, it looks like he's getting lucky tonight."

They walked toward the bar where Wild Card stood, a woman facing him, his arm around her waist holding her close to him. He leaned in and murmured something against the woman's ear.

Steele couldn't see her face, but everything about her

reminded him of Laurie. Her long, dark hair, waves cascading around her shoulders. Her slender but shapely frame. Even the way she would dress if she weren't wearing Raven's clothes. Lean jeans that accentuated her tight, round ass. A lacy camisole leaving her shoulders bare.

She laughed at whatever Wild Card had said to her and he would have sworn that was Laurie's laugh.

Fuck, he had it bad.

Wild Card's gaze lifted from the woman he seemed intent on charming to them.

"Steele, hey, look who I ran into."

The woman turned around and . . . fuck, it was like a slam to the chest. It *was* Laurie.

"What the hell are you doing here?"

At his sharp words, the soft, enchanting smile that had spread across her face at seeing him faded.

"I wanted to see you again."

"Laurie, you and I are done. There's no reason for you to be here, so why don't you just go back to your cozy little town house and—"

"I'm selling it."

"What?"

"And I've quit my job."

"Why the fuck did you do that?"

She shook her head. "Donovan got me that job. It was with one of his companies. And he got me a good price on the town house because his business had dealings with the builder." She shrugged. "I wouldn't have been able to afford it without the job anyway." She stared into Steele's eyes. "Everything there reminded me of Donovan. How I'd allowed myself to be convinced he was good for me. That he cared for me. Then later, how I allowed him to control me." She sipped her drink. "So I walked away."

"I'm sorry. I got the impression you loved that place."

She nodded. "I did." And she locked gazes with him. "But I'll love again."

His chest tightened, but he took a deep drag of his beer. "So what are you going to do now?"

"I was hoping that . . ." She pursed her lips. "Well, that I could ride with you."

He shook his head. "I already told you. You and I can't be together."

"I know," she said hesitantly, "but I really think riding with you, all of you, would clear my head and help me figure out what to do next. Wild Card said I could ride with him."

Steele glared at Wild Card, who simply sipped his beer innocently.

"I think we should let Laurie ride with us." Dom's eyes glinted as he stared at Steele, his lips turning up in a grin.

"It's not your call," Steele said, his fists clenching at his sides.

"Now, wait," Rip said. "As much as you're the leader, Steele, and we all respect that, what the rest of us want should count for something."

Steele's gaze shot to Rip. What the hell was he saying?

Rip rested his hand on Steele's shoulder and guided him a few steps away.

"Look, you say you aren't in love with her, and you ended things on good terms. If that's all true, then you shouldn't have any problem with her riding with us."

Blinding anger flared through Steele, but he knew he wouldn't win this. The men were clearly hatching a scheme to get him and Laurie together again.

"Fuck, do whatever the hell you want." He turned on his heel and stormed toward the door.

He just hoped the guys wouldn't be flung off his fists before this whole thing was over.

As Steele sped along the highway, he was totally aware of Laurie only yards away. She was riding with Wild Card, her arms around his waist, her body tight against him. He remembered how that felt, and longed to feel her soft, warm body against him again. And not just on the back of his bike. His cock twitched.

When they got back to the cottage where they were staying, Steele went straight up to bed.

He could hear the others laughing and drinking. At one point, he heard splashing in the lake, which was right near the cottage, and he itched to look out the window and see if Laurie was skinny-dipping with Wild Card. But she was just riding with Wild Card. They weren't together.

But that didn't mean she wouldn't fuck him. She wasn't with Steele anymore. She could fuck anyone she wanted. Maybe she was out there fucking all of them.

His gut clenched. He knew his imagination was just

going wild. Because he missed her. Because he wanted her to be his.

He tried to ignore his raging emotions and closed his eyes.

For a while he dozed off, but he awoke to the sound of soft moans. His eyelids snapped open. It was in the room next to his.

Fuck, that was Wild Card's room. He was in there with Laurie.

His cock was gliding into her. He was making her come.

Before he knew what had happened, Steele was on his feet and out the door. He tried the doorknob to Wild Card's room, but it was locked, so he stepped back and, using a powerful side kick, slammed his heel into the door. The wood of the frame splintered and the door swung open. He stormed inside, seeing the couple in the shadowy room, and he grabbed Wild Card's arm and yanked him off of Laurie.

Except the man was Rip, not Wild Card.

His gaze shot to the naked woman lying on the bed, her long, dark hair spread across the white pillowcase.

Raven grinned at him. "Steele, I know you're feeling lonely, but just wait until we're finished, okay?"

"I thought . . ."

Rip took his arm and guided him to a nearby chair. "We know what you thought, but we switched rooms with Wild Card yesterday, remember?"

"So where's Laurie?" Steele demanded.

"She's bunking in with Wild Card."

He glared at Rip.

Rip's eyebrow arched. "So are you going to go break into his room now?"

"Yeah, don't do that, Steele," Raven said.

"Sorry, Raven," Steele bit out, anger and adrenaline causing his heart to beat out of control. "I didn't mean to interrupt."

He stood up and headed to the door, his pulse slowing as he collected himself. The frame was broken, but Rip pushed the door into place and it sounded like he dragged a chair against it to prop it closed. Steele didn't want to go back to his room and hear them fucking again, so he headed downstairs to get a drink.

He walked through the dark living room, lit only by the moonlight glowing in the window. As he walked into the hallway leading to the kitchen, he bumped into a shadowy figure walking toward him.

From the softness and height, he already knew this was Laurie, but the warmth of her body against his, and the scent of her hair, knocked his senses into turmoil. From the shimmering moonlight, he could see she wore just an oversized T-shirt, and he could imagine the outline of her nipples showing through the fabric.

The hallway was narrow and he pressed her to the wall, breathing in her intoxicating scent.

"Laurie."

"Steele." Her hands were flat against his chest as she gazed up at him. He couldn't see her features, but he could see the glitter of her eyes in the scant moonlight.

He couldn't help himself. He lowered his face to hers and captured her lips. Then he moaned at the sweetness of her soft, yielding mouth. His tongue glided inside her and he thought he'd die of pleasure.

He cupped her round ass, which was naked under the thin cloth of her nightshirt, and pulled her tight to his groin. She moaned as his hard cock pressed against her.

The way she looked at him . . . the way her soft body felt against him . . . He wanted to brush her hair from her face. To kiss her with sweet, tender passion.

Fuck, who was he kidding? He wanted to shove her up against the wall and drive into her, deep and hard. To fuck her so hard, she'd have no doubt she was his, and his alone.

Which is exactly why he had to let go of her. Right now.

He stepped back.

"Fuck, why did you come back?" he muttered, trying to control his raging emotions.

An awkward silence hung between them.

"Steele—"

At the sound of footsteps on the stairs, then a giggle, she glanced around, smoothing down her nightshirt.

Steele turned and headed to the hallway, Laurie trailing behind him. As they entered the hall, Raven headed toward them, Rip in tow.

"We're hungry. Just coming to make a sandwich," Raven said cheerfully.

Rip just nodded in greeting.

Steele returned the nod and passed them silently. Laurie followed him up the stairs and when they reached his door, they stopped.

He wanted to drag her into his room, and his bed. To ravage her all night long.

Fool that he was.

Laurie gazed at him. She wanted him to ask her into his room. Into his bed.

She longed to sleep curled up in his arms.

When she'd come here, she'd known it would take time to convince him. But now . . . having to walk away from him in this dark hallway . . . almost broke her heart.

"Steele, I want to be honest with you."

He frowned. "I'm listening."

"The reason I came here is because . . ." She gazed up at him, willing him to believe in them. "I want a chance to convince you that we can work. I don't want you to hold back. I mean, maybe be a bit patient with me, but I want you to dominate me. What Donovan did, that was abuse. What you do . . . it's exciting and sexy." She took his hand and held it within her own. "And I know you would never hurt me."

His face was grim and he drew his hand from her grip. "I already proved to you that it won't work."

"But that's not fair. You were trying to push me too hard."

He leaned close, his intimidating presence backing her against the wall. "Who said I was fair? When I dominate a woman, she does exactly what I tell her to do, when I tell her to do it. And she likes it. No questions. No whining. Just blind submission." He glared at her. "If you can't do that, then it won't work."

He was still trying to scare her, to push her away. She knew that. But unfortunately, he was succeeding.

Had it been a mistake coming here?

Her stomach twisted and she turned away, then headed for the door to the room she shared with Wild Card.

Steele watched Laurie walk down the dark hall and open the bedroom door, then slip inside. His gut clenched at the thought that she'd be climbing into bed with another man.

He went into his room and closed the door, then slumped onto the bed. With his hands behind his head, he stared at the white ceiling above, visible in the soft glow of moonlight. Laurie was probably snuggling up beside Wild Card right now, her soft body close to his.

Fuck! He rolled over, glowering in the darkness.

It's not like she and Wild Card were together. But, damn it, the man wasn't made of stone. With Laurie close and soft in his bed, why wouldn't he make love to her? He'd already fucked her before when they'd been sharing.

It would be meaningless, just physical intimacy. But it wasn't meaningless to Steele. The thought of Wild Card touching her drove him insane with jealousy.

God damn it, Steele loved her. He'd known it all along. But he couldn't be with her. He couldn't take a chance on hurting her.

But his heart ached with need. If only she would come over here right now. Slide into his bed and tell him again that they could work things out. Right now, maybe he'd actually believe her. Because he wanted it so badly.

With her help . . . maybe they *could* make it work.

A knock sounded at the door and his heart stopped.

"Come in." He sat up and turned on the light on the bedside table as the door opened. Was it Laurie?

"Hey, there," Raven said, peering in at him. "May I come in?"

"Yeah, of course."

Raven closed the door and walked to the bed, then sat on the edge.

"I thought you might want to talk," she said.

He shrugged. "About what?"

She rolled her eyes. "You are such a guy. About Laurie, of course."

Raven leaned toward him. "Why don't you try telling her how you feel?"

He raised an eyebrow. "And how do I feel?"

"You're crazy about her. And either you're denying that to yourself, or you've found some reason why you think it won't work."

"Rave, leave it alone."

She pursed her lips. "If I actually thought you meant that, I would. But you have that lost little-boy look and I know you just need to be pushed in the right direction." She leaned in close. "Why don't you tell me why you're fighting this?"

He stared into her stubborn face and knew he wouldn't get away with shrugging this off.

"You know what she's been through. The last thing she needs is a domineering jerk like me controlling her in the bedroom."

Raven laughed. "Oh, is that all? I thought this was something serious."

"Raven."

"No, you listen to me. You are big, intimidating, and possessive."

"You're not making things better."

"And you are protective, loving, and caring. She couldn't hope for a better man. She knows . . . we all know . . . that you will take care of her. And protect her." She jabbed him in the chest with a fingertip. "Even from you."

He didn't share her confidence.

"If I start to dominate her—"

"What, you'll scare her? That girl doesn't scare easily."

"But what if I go too far? What if I hurt her?"

Her face softened with a smile. "You would never do that. You've been dominating women for a long time. You can sense what they want and what they don't want." Her eyebrow quirked up. "And she can speak up, you know. She's not just going to lie there and let you hurt her. If you get out of line, I'm sure she'll call you on it." She tipped her head. "Have you ever gone too far with a woman?"

"Of course not."

"Okay."

"But she was abused."

"And so she's definitely going to push back. I've gotten to know Laurie and she's not going to let anyone treat her the way that rat-bastard did again."

She patted his hand. "Well, think about it."

Then she stood up and strolled to the door. She opened it and glanced over her shoulder. "Have a good night."

Steele turned out the light and lay in the darkness thinking about what Raven had said. Could he make this thing work between him and Laurie?

Fuck, he wanted to so badly he could taste it.

Laurie lay in the bed beside Wild Card. When he'd volunteered to help her with this plan to win Steele back, he'd offered to give her the bed while he slept on a sleeping bag on the floor, but she'd insisted he share the bed with her.

In his sleep, Wild Card had rolled over and slid his arm around her, then drew her close. Now she was tight against his hot, hard body and she could feel his cock swelling against her thigh.

Clearly, she hadn't really thought it through.

He murmured softly then nuzzled her ear. His hand started to wander from her waist upward.

"Wild Card," she whispered.

"Mmm. Yeah, baby." His hand cupped her breast. She knew he wasn't really awake and was just responding to a woman in his bed.

The feel of his big, warm hand on her was comforting . . . and stimulating.

But all she could think of was Steele.

He stroked her breast, then slid to the other, his lips caressing her neck now.

She turned her head to face him. "Wild Card?"

His eyelids opened, and he blinked. Then he slid his hand away. "Aw, sorry, Laurie. I didn't mean to—"

"I know."

Wild Card started to turn away, but she grasped his muscular bicep.

"Don't go." She gazed at him with wide eyes, not quite sure what she was asking for. She just knew she wanted him close. She needed to feel wanted right now.

He slid his arm around her waist again. "Whatever you want, you've got it." He smiled. "You're just a little confused right now, but don't worry. I'm sure Steele will come around."

She gazed into his hazel eyes, so filled with warmth and understanding. She rested her hand on his raspy cheek, then stroked it. "Thank you."

She felt so close to him right now. She cupped his face between her hands, insecurity and need building in her. She leaned toward him and brushed her lips against his, then deepened the kiss.

She could almost imagine he was Steele. Even though she knew it was wrong, she wanted . . . no, needed . . . this closeness. She slid her tongue into his mouth and sighed softly.

Wild Card drew back and gazed into her eyes. "I know you think you want this right now, but we both know that you're Steele's woman."

"You're fucking right about that."

Laurie's gaze darted to where Steele stood staring at them from the open doorway.

"Laurie, are you my woman or not?" Steele demanded.

Her eyes widened and she sat up in bed. "I . . . uh . . ."

"Yes or no?"

"Yes!" She gazed at Wild Card in apology, but he just grinned.

"Then get into my room and into bed." Steele's glittering granite gaze brooked no argument.

She pushed back the covers and scurried across the room, joy bursting through her, then ducked under Steele's arm that gripped the door, and down the hall.

Steele glanced toward Wild Card and nodded. "Thanks."

Wild Card chuckled. "Anytime. Now go take care of your woman."

Steele turned and strode to his room. Laurie was sitting in bed, the covers around her, staring at him with her big blue eyes. He shoved the door closed behind him.

"That was a dangerous game you were playing. Didn't you care that I might beat the living daylights out of Wild Card?"

She shook her head. "I knew you wouldn't do that."

"Why?" he demanded.

"Because you know I'm not in any danger from Wild Card. And you respect him, and all your men, too much."

He walked toward her, keeping his expression stern. "You think you know me better than I know myself?"

Her eyes widened as he approached, but she didn't cringe as he strode closer. "I know that you're a good man, and I know that you would never hurt me, or any of your crew."

He sat down on the bed beside her, then curled his fingers around her cheek and grasped her face. "You got that right."

Then he captured her lips, delving his tongue inside. Claiming her. Deeply and thoroughly. When he released her lips, she sucked in a breath.

He smiled. He loved leaving her breathless.

"So you're going to ride with us?"

She nodded.

"And have sex with every one of my crew?" he said with a teasing grin.

Laurie laughed at the gleam in his granite eyes. "Depends on whether or not I'm in the mood. And right now? I'm definitely in the mood. Should I go back and do that for Wild Card right now?"

He laughed and rolled her onto her back, then prowled over her.

"Fuck, no. Right now I want you right here."

She felt his big heavy cock glide across her belly, then he ripped off her panties and dipped his finger into her folds. He pressed his cockhead against her slit and slowly pushed inside, his gaze locked on hers the whole time he filled her with his considerable length.

The welcome feel of being stretched by his generous girth sent her heart pumping faster.

Once he was fully immersed in her, he lay still, watching her.

Finally, she groaned. "Please, for God's sake, fuck me."

He laughed, then pulled back and glided deep again. She squeezed around him.

He nipped her ear. "Tell me you want me."

She smiled. "I want you."

He drew back and glided forward again, sending tremors through her.

"Tell me how much."

Her smile softened and she stroked his cheek. "You are my world. I want you so much it's indescribable." She kissed his raspy chin. "I love you, and I'd do anything to be with you."

His eyes gleamed and he leaned in and kissed her.

"Oh, God, baby. I love you, too."

Then he thrust deeply again, making her gasp.

She clutched his shoulders and arched her hips against him. He was deep inside her, but it wasn't deep enough. She wanted him to consume her. She wanted to be one with him.

He thrust, and thrust again.

"Oh, God, Steele." Tears welled from her eyes.

He kept thrusting. Filling her with his massive cock.

Pleasure swelled and she clung to him, riding the waves
of bliss.

"Fuck, baby, I'm so close."

"Come for me, Steele. Fill me."

He groaned, then she felt hot semen erupt inside her.
She gasped, and catapulted to heaven, moaning his name.

He kept driving into her, faster and faster, until her
moans faded to soft whimpers of pleasure, and finally she
sighed, sated. He stroked the hair from her face and smiled,
then kissed her tenderly.

"You are one hot fuck, you know that?"

But the warmth in his eyes glowed with love, contra-
dicting his rough words.

She smacked his perfectly sculpted ass and laughed. "So
are you."

He rolled back and pulled her on top of him. She wasn't
ready to end this, and she was sure he wasn't either, so she
sat up and stroked her breasts. As she pinched her nipples,
his stiffening cock turned to steel inside her.

She began to move her hips, loving the feel of him between her legs. Riding him like a big, powerful bike.

"Now that I've got you where I want you, tell me
again," she said.

He smiled. "I love you. I will always love you."

She giggled, feeling giddy. Then she rode him even
harder. Soon another orgasm swelled through her and she
moaned, her whole body trembling.

And before long, he let loose a primal growl and then
erupted inside her again.

Finally, she dropped onto the bed beside him, and he pulled her into his arms and kissed her soundly.

"You know I'm never going to let you go."

She laughed. "I'm counting on it."

Epilogue

"So where are we going, Raven?" Laurie asked.

Raven had suggested the two of them go shopping and for some reason Shock had gone with them. But instead of going to the cute boutiques along the main street that Laurie had expected, Raven and Shock had led her down a side street to an old house.

"You said you'd like to do something to surprise Steele."

"That's true. I thought I might get him a chain."

Raven shrugged. "Yeah, you could do that, but wouldn't you rather do something more special?"

"I know he really likes this one chain."

Raven smiled. "But I was thinking more personal. And, Shock and I have just the idea."

"You and Shock?"

"Yes. He knows a guy. And trust me, Steele will be more than a little excited if you do this. Right, Shock?"

"I'd be sporting a huge boner if a chick did this for me."

Raven laughed, giving Shock a long, languid look. "I think you're sporting a boner just thinking about it."

Laurie quivered. She wasn't sure what they were suggesting as Shock rapped on the front door, but when it opened, the toughest, and at the same time, most stunning, intensely sexy man, opened the door. His head was shaved and he was naked from the waist up, revealing his densely inked torso and arms. He didn't smile, but his hawklike gaze locked on her and perused her from head to toe, and everywhere in between, with laser intensity, sending a tingle of awareness fluttering through her.

He glanced at Shock and nodded. "Come in."

Then he turned and walked inside. His entire back, arms, and even up his neck and onto this scalp, was tattooed. He was one badass-looking man.

He led them past a pristinely clean kitchen, then down a hallway. Oh, God, was he taking her to a bedroom?

Laurie glanced nervously at Raven and Shock. What exactly did they have in mind?

Was the idea that he would teach her some sexual technique that she could then perform with Steele?

"Are you leaving me with this man?" she murmured to Raven.

Raven patted her arm. "Of course not. I wouldn't leave you alone to do this." She smiled. "In fact, I'm doing it, too. In this, just like you, I'm a virgin."

"I'm doing it, too, but I'm no virgin," Shock said.

The four of them were doing it together? What kind

of kinky thing did they have in mind, and why wouldn't they just have Steele here with her?

Maybe it was something Steele would like to watch her do and they were going to make a video.

When Laurie stepped into the room, the man turned, and as soon as she saw his equipment, she sucked in a breath as she now understood what they intended. "I don't think I can do this."

"Sure you can, love," the man said. "It'll hurt at first, but it'll be worth it." His pearly white smile did nothing to diminish the dangerous edge to his tough, good looks. "Now unzip those tight jeans of yours and turn around. I'm dying to see that sexy ass of yours."

She glanced at Raven and then at Shock. They both smiled in encouragement.

She unzipped her jeans and lowered them as the man stepped up behind her.

"By the way," he said as his fingertips came to rest on her hip, then glided across and down a few inches of her ass. "They call me Razor." He chuckled as she stiffened under his touch. "But don't worry. I won't draw too much blood."

Steele tossed in a handful of poker chips and smiled at Magic. "I call."

Rip, Wild Card, and Dom had already folded. When Magic revealed his cards, Steele chuckled and showed his winning hand—three kings—then raked in the hefty pile of chips from the center of the table.

At the sound of the front door opening, he glanced up. Laurie came into the living room, followed by Raven and Shock.

"Where have you all been?" Rip asked, glancing at Raven.

She grinned. "I have a surprise for you." She linked arms with Laurie and giggled. "We went and did something neither of us has ever done before and . . ." She giggled again. "We think you and Steele are going to like it."

"If it was you two in a threesome with Shock, I would have liked to watch," Rip said with a grin.

"Well, there was another man," Raven admitted. "Someone Shock introduced us to."

This time, Rip frowned at Shock. "What other man?"

"His name was Razor," Raven said.

Steele glanced at Rip, who returned his perplexed look. The way they were behaving, Steele wasn't sure what to think.

Steele's eyebrow arched. "What did you do, Laurie?"

"Well, it was the three of us," Laurie said, clearly anxious as her gaze shifted from him to Raven.

"And Razor," he said, anger building within him at the thought of a stranger touching her.

Laurie pursed her lips. "Yes, Razor, too."

"Who the hell is Razor?" Steele demanded, wondering exactly what this Razor dude had done to his woman.

"Razor is your next best friend," Shock said, "when you find out what he's done."

"Fuck, just tell me!" Steele said.

Raven squeezed Laurie's arm. "You could show him and everyone else right here, but maybe the first time, you want to do it somewhere more private."

Laurie nodded. "You're right." She gazed at Steele. "I can show the others another time. This first time is special for you."

"Well, now we're all curious," Wild Card said with a grin.

"Don't worry. Once the girls have shared with their men, then the three of us will show you together," Shock said.

Steele's stomach clenched as Laurie led him upstairs, on the heels of Raven and Rip, who'd raced up ahead of them. He stepped into the bedroom after her and she closed the door, then looked at him a bit nervously.

"I hope you don't get mad. I mean, I think you'll like it. A lot."

"Just tell me."

"I really need to show you." She unfastened the button of her jeans, then undid the zipper.

He frowned. What exactly was she going to show him? Some unusual sexual act? Something that she'd done with Raven, Shock, and another guy?

"Why did you go to this Razor guy? Couldn't you have done whatever it is with us here?"

She frowned and shook her head. "No one here has the equipment or the skill."

Steele pushed back his shoulders, frowning. "I think I've proven my skill often enough and—"

But his words stopped as his gaze locked on Laurie's sexy ass as she revealed it. She gazed over her shoulder at him with a smile.

On her right butt cheek was a patch of gauze. The tightness in his stomach eased.

"Will you do the honors?" she asked.

He stepped toward her and gently peeled away the tape holding the gauze in place, then drew it back.

"What do you think?"

A jolt of delight burst through him at the sight of the cutest little biker chick in bright colored ink tattooed on her ass. He laughed heartily.

"Raven and I decided to call her Bebe," Laurie said, "for Biker Babe."

He grinned. "You both got one done?"

She nodded. "I wanted to do something special for you. To show you how committed I am to you and the crew."

He dragged his finger along the top of her ass cheek, above the red, slightly swollen flesh around the tattoo. "I love it!"

Then he tipped his head. "Shock said he did it, too?"

"Oh, yeah, he got another tattoo, but not Bebe. He got a tribal design on his arm."

Steele chuckled. "Okay. That makes more sense."

He crouched down and took a close look at Bebe, the new woman in his life. One he looked forward to exploring intimately . . . once she was fully healed. He imagined licking her from head to toe, including her sexy bike.

"She really is one sexy babe." He stood up and turned Laurie around to face him.

Laurie started to pull up her jeans and Steele stopped her. "Not so fast. I don't think you're going to be needing those on right now."

"You know that my ass hurts, right?"

"That's okay," he said as he took her hand and walked backward toward the bed. "You can be on top."

"I see." She grinned.

He sat on the edge of the bed and she kissed him, then flattened her palm on his chest and pushed him back. He watched as she dropped her jeans to the floor and shed her undies. As she prowled over him on the bed she grinned. She unzipped his jeans and pulled out his already growing cock, then stroked it.

"Mmm. The sight of Bebe sure has made you hard." She leaned forward and licked him, then prowled over him and pressed him to her opening. "I guess Bebe and I are going to spend a lot of time riding Steele!"

Fulfill all your wildest fantasies with **Opal Carew**...

• *Twin Fantasies* • *Swing*
• *Blush* • *Six* • *Secret Ties* • *Forbidden Heat*
• *Bliss* • *Pleasure Bound* • *Total Abandon*
• *Secret Weapon* • *Insatiable* • *Illicit*
• *His to Command* • *His to Possess*
• *His to Claim* • *Riding Steele*

AVAILABLE JULY 2015 *Hard Ride*

"Beautiful erotic romance...real and powerful."
—*RT BookReviews*